Christy Wilburn Nobella Webb

Secrets
of the
Old
Music
Room

BOOK 2

MILDRED'S REVENGE

STRATTON
—PRESS—
Publishing Life

Secrets of the Old Music Room
Copyright © 2018 **Christy Wilburn Nobella Webb**

Stratton Press, LLC
1603 Capitol Ave, Suite 310,
Cheyenne, WY 82001
www.stratton-press.com
1-888-323-7009

ISBN (Paperback): 978-1-64345-143-5
ISBN (Ebook): 978-1-64345-144-2

Printed in the United States of America

Dedicated to my sister, Sylvia, who always encouraged me to write and has lovingly given me financial support to make my writing dreams possible, and to my loving husband, Dean Webb, who loves and supports me in my writing! Thank you!

I hope music lovers will enjoy the play on the musical words throughout the book!

Prologue

August 1968
Salt Lake City, Utah

It began as an ordinary day for Debra Wilkin, who volunteered to water her grandfather's yard while he was on vacation. She enjoyed going to his home and had always considered it to be a little old fashioned due to its floor plan. His home was a duplex where the kitchen door exited onto a landing that had a short flight of stairs placing you into the garage. Once in the garage, you could turn right to a door that led outside to the backyard, or you could turn left and go down another flight of stairs that led to the basement door of the old **music** room, where this story takes place.

Debra idolized her grandfather and especially admired his gift for **music**. His living room consisted of a **baby grand piano** on the north end and a beautiful **organ** on the south end. His **musical talent** also included the ability to **play** the **harmonica** and a knack for storytelling. With the passing of Grandmother Herman, her grandfather started a new hobby of building and crafting **violins** and grandfather clocks to help fill his lonely hours. Due to his love for **music**, he had always encouraged each of his grandchildren to develop their **musical talents**, promising that whoever worked the hardest would one day inherit his **baby grand piano**. Debra secretly hoped that lucky grandchild would be her.

On Debra's first day of watering, she had brought a knitting project to help pass the time while she waited for the watering stations to finish. Instead of working on her knitting, she decided to go downstairs to explore the old **music** room. She was thrilled when she found the door unlocked and held her breath slightly when the door made a creaking noise, announcing her arrival. After turning on the light, she took in the large, spacious room, admiring the variety of souvenir hats hung carefully on the walls as a reminder of the many places her grandfather has traveled to.

On another wall was an old-fashioned **pump organ**; however, her favorite item in the room was the old **player piano** in the far north corner. She would never forget the first time she saw her grandfather **play** this **piano**; his feet were pumping the **pedals** vigorously, and then beautiful **music** began to magically flow out of the **instrument** while invisible hands **played** the **keys**. He had made it perfectly clear to all his grandchildren that they were not to touch or **play** this **piano** without first getting his permission.

Debra couldn't resist the urge to go and just sit at the **piano**. While sitting and admiring the splendid **piano**, happy memories began flooding her mind, and it seemed like the **piano** was begging her to touch its **keys** to draw out the enchanting **music**. She tried several times to pump the **pedals** like she had seen her grandfather do, without success. She stood and slid the bench forward, and without even realizing it, her fingers triggered a mechanism underneath the **keyboard paneling** that caused the **piano** to awaken and begin **playing** an unusual **tune**. Within seconds, the **keys** began to depress, and without warning, an apparition of **notes** suddenly began floating up and out of the top of the **piano** and soon began swirling around her. She immediately wished she hadn't touched the **piano** and wasn't sure what to do to make the **notes** go away. Too frightened to move, she watched as the **notes** continued to circle and take on the form of a person.

To Debra's surprise, a middle-aged man with a receding hairline and a round, chubby face appeared and introduced himself as none other than **Middle C**. His physique was pear shaped, and he wore an immaculate tuxedo with tails. Removing his hat, he bowed, which caused the buttons on his tuxedo to creak and groan as they stretched to accommodate his scrupulous bow. Even more astonishing was the question he asked her, "I am **Middle C** at your service. You beckoned me. How may I be of service?"

Feeling quite shocked at the situation before her, she finally managed to ask, "Are you like a genie?"

"Good heavens no!" **Middle C** quickly replied. "I don't grant silly wishes. I am here to educate and support your **musical vocation**. Please get on with your request. I have others I need to serve as well."

Not having any idea of what to suggest, Debra finally used the excuse that she had to water the yard and couldn't go because she would get into a lot of trouble if she flooded things while being gone. **Middle C** quickly informed her that when they traveled, regular time stood still, so there wasn't any need for her to worry about the yard flooding. With no more excuses, Debra agreed to take her first adventure on **Middle C's** **music** mobile. To her amazement, she watched as **Middle C** pulled an antique **metronome** from one of his inside jacket pockets and began twisting various knobs. The unusual **music** began to **play** again, and soon the flurry of **notes** encircled them, delivering them to the **music** mobile.

The best way to describe the **music** mobile was to compare it to an enlarged golf cart that could accommodate seating a dozen or so easily. It had an attached ceiling, with open sides where one could look out and observe the scenery and movement surrounding it while traveling. When looking down at the ground, you could tell you were flying; however, it wasn't easy to determine how high or fast you were going since you couldn't see homes or cars or even trees like you would if you were flying in an airplane. She watched in fascination as **Middle C** reached into another inside pocket of his tuxedo and pulled out a **baton**, which he began waving to organize the **notes** that had delivered them into the **music** mobile. Once they were in a perfect **synchronized pattern**, it allowed the **music** mobile to begin to glide forward. When she looked out the side of the **music** mobile, she could see **notes** moving in all directions; some **notes** seemed to be in a big hurry while others drifted about, taking their sweet time. It appeared that there were **musical** intersections similar to the intersections you would have if you were driving. Instead of traffic lights, there were **conductors leading** the traffic of **notes**. If you **listened** closely, you could hear a variety of **melodies harmonizing** as each took their turn in the procession.

Middle C advised Debra that they had one more passenger to pick up and stopped at a **whole rest** stop for a **short interlude**. While waiting, she could still feel the constant **pulsating beats** of the **melody** while the **notes** continued to keep up with the catchy **rhythm**. Hearing footsteps and feeling a slight rocking **movement** of the **music** mobile, she looked up to see a handsome young man progressing her way. She was immediately caught off guard by his good looks—raven-black hair, large brown eyes, and an incredible white smile—and it seemed that her **vocal cords** had decided to freeze up on her when he asked her name.

Despite his handsome looks and well-built body, Ted had been snubbed before by pretty girls due to the fact that he did janitorial work. He assumed that Debra was acting like all the other pretty girls he had encountered, and a fiery exchange of words began to take place when she didn't immediately answer him. After calling a truce, they slowly got back to communicating civilly with each other; however, they were both still on guard.

Debra was curious about how Ted had met **Middle C**. He explained that they had met one day while he was cleaning the **music** room at the junior high school when he had tried to blow **notes** out of a **tuba**. It surprised Debra to **learn** that he didn't **play** an **instrument**, and she couldn't help asking him how he knew so much about **music**. Ted had a secret and wasn't about to share it with a girl he had just met, in spite of how beautiful her sapphire-blue eyes sparkled and how her gorgeous strawberry-blonde hair hung enticingly around her shoulders. When asked further about not **playing** an **instrument**, he answered rather defensively that as much as he would like to be in the **band** and drive a fancy car, he wasn't born with a silver spoon in his mouth.

Middle C revealed Ted's secret to Debra, and she found out firsthand what an incredible **tenor voice** he had. She further discovered that **Middle C** had a plan for her to break down Ted's barrier walls and persuade him to open up and **sing** again so the world could hear and enjoy his glorious **tenor voice**. She and Ted were whisked away to a **music conservatory** twice a week, where they were enrolled with four other **talented music students** to develop their **musical abilities**. No one knew what the other students' **talents** were because they **practiced** in **soundproof learning** rooms. After several weeks of **practice**, they were each given a chance to **perform** in order to advance to the next level. Those that participate**d** were rewarded with unbelievable opportunities.

While attending the **conservatory**, Debra noticed a rival for Ted's attention by another student, Rita. It was obvious that Rita came from a very affluent background, always coming to class dressed to perfection in the latest fashions. It appeared she was accustomed to getting her way with any guy she went after, and she blatantly flirted with Ted, trying to win his attention. She even went so far as to telephone Ted and brag to Debra that she was the luckiest girl alive to be enrolled at the **conservatory** and insinuated that Ted has been making romantic phone calls to her.

Debra pled with **Middle C** to take her home; however, **Middle C** used this opportunity to strand her with Ted while he fixed a temporary malfunction of his **metronome**. Ted explained to Debra that he had tried to tell her about Rita's phone call; however, due to their always being in a rush to get to class, he didn't get a chance to finish telling her what really happened. They shared their first kiss, and a bond of trust and love began growing between them. They promised to always be honest with each other in order to prevent a misunderstanding in the future.

While waiting for **Middle C** to return to pick them up, Debra coaxed Ted to **play** a "guess that **tune**" game, where he finally revealed his incredible **voice** to her. She was fully aware of his **talent** due to hearing him **sing** previously, but she knew that he was not aware of it. He agreed to **play**; however, in the process, he began putting up his barrier walls. Debra quickly reminded him of their agreement to be honest and was able to get him to open up and share the hurt he had held in for years. This experience had enabled Ted to find the joy in his **singing** again, and he invited Debra to a Fourth of July **per-**

formance, where he **sang** a **medley** of patriotic **songs** at the White House.

Debra was having the time of her life and didn't want it to end. She had mixed emotions over her grandfather coming home from his vacation because she wouldn't be needed to water his yards. Her mother came up with a perfect solution of asking him for a job to clean his home on a weekly basis. She was excited to meet with him, but nervous about having to tell him she touched his **player piano** without asking his permission first. With Ted's encouragement, she knew what she had to do and was working up the courage to be honest to tell her grandfather everything. To her complete surprise, when she showed her grandfather how she summoned **Middle C**, she discovered that they have been friends for years! Her grandfather also attended the **conservatory** and had always hoped that one of his children or grandchildren would follow in his footsteps. He talked to her mother and conveniently **arranged** for her to continue coming over to his home several times during the week.

Everything seemed to be going perfect—that was until Mildred decided she wanted to marry her grandfather. Debra was happy at first that her grandfather had found someone he could spend time with and had tried on several occasions to become friends with her. It seemed that Mildred had her own agenda, and it didn't include being friends with Debra. Mildred picked up quickly on the fact that something was going on in the old **music** room, and it had something to do with the **player piano**. On a return trip back to her grandfather's home in the **music** mobile, **Middle C** and Debra caught Mildred snooping around the **player piano** and even going through Debra's personal bag. **Middle C** had no other choice but to use his fairy dust to prevent Mildred from seeing their arrival. When Debra suddenly appeared and confronted Mildred, she was startled and demanded to know what's going on. She further threatened Debra that she knew something was going on and when she and Debra's grandfather got married, the first thing to go would be the **player piano**!

Chapter 1

Debra sat nervously in an uncomfortable chair waiting for her turn to **perform** in the **piano recital**. Why was her body torturing her with a merciless case of nerves while her mind was fighting to reassure her she didn't have anything to be worried about? While trying desperately to divert her attention away from her torturous nerves, she thought about Ted and wondered where he was and what he was doing. She remembered the roses he had given her the day of their first **performance** at the **conservatory** and him telling her they would bring her good luck. When she recalled how they had brought her good luck, she smiled and wished that she was holding those roses now. Her thoughts were suddenly interrupted with the **sound** of **applause**, and she looked up to see her **piano teacher** waving her forward for her turn to **perform**. Taking a deep breath to calm her frayed nerves, she stood and followed Mrs. Hocking as they walked out on to the stage.

"I am pleased to **introduce** my next **student**, Debra Wilkin, who has **studied** with me for many years. Please join me in welcoming her to the stage," Mrs. Hocking announced.

"Good evening, ladies and gentlemen. It is my pleasure to **perform** for you 'Clarese le Dune' by Clyde Debosney." Settling herself at the **piano**, she remembered that soon she would be traveling to meet Mr. Debosney, and compared to **playing** for him, this was a **piece** of cake! With those thoughts tucked safely in her mind, she stretched her fingers, willing them to relax and then began calmly **playing** the **notes**, falling in love all over again with the romantic and sentimental **piece**. Lost in the beauty of the **music**, she soon forgot she had an **audience** and **played** as if she were **performing** for Mr. Debosney, remembering to **pause** and embellish each section the way he had intended it to be **played**. Finishing the final **runs** of the **song**, her heart was content with the ending **notes**, **listening** intently as the **notes vibrated** their way from the front of the stage to the last seat of the **auditorium**. The **applause** was thunderous, and her heart was instantly filled with emotion as she graciously stood and faced the **audience**, curtsying in acknowledgment of their appreciation for her **performance.**

"Wow, **Middle C**, can you believe the way Debra can **play** the **piano**?" Ted asked.

"I don't think Clyde could have **performed** any better," **Middle C** responded in agreement.

"Thanks again for bringing me to her **recital**. I'm glad she doesn't know we're here, or she probably would have really been nervous. Being a speck of dust is amazing, **Middle C**. I could get used to traveling around like this!"

"Well, dear boy, it's only used for special occasions such as this, not to be overdone."

"I hope she gets the roses I left for her. Can we at least stick around and make sure she gets them before we have to leave?"

"I suppose so." **Middle C** sighed while looking inside his tuxedo for his trusty **metronome**.

"Debra, your **performance** was remarkable. It was absolutely flawless and perfection itself! Oh, before I forget, these were delivered for you right after you went out to **perform**," Mrs. Hocking replied, handing her the beautiful bunch of roses.

When Debra looked at the roses, she couldn't believe her eyes when she saw the colors of red, white, blue, and peach, which were the exact same colors Ted had given her the day she **performed** at the **conservatory**. He hadn't forgotten her! Reaching for the card, her hands shook with excitement as she opened it and read,

Wish I could be there with you, Debra. Hope these roses bring you as much success as they did before. You're in my heart and thoughts.

Love,
Ted

Tears filled her eyes as she thought about Ted while rereading the card. Oh, how she loved and missed him. She suddenly turned and looked up at the ceiling, sensing his presence for a brief moment. She remembered the time she and **Middle C** had **listened** to him, disguised like a fly on the wall, and wondered if he had been in attendance at her **recital**. Smiling, she said, "If you're up there, Ted, thank you!"

"**Middle C**, can she see us?" Ted asked nervously.

"No, Theodore. However, she may have briefly felt our presence. Time to go. We must be on our way now, **pronto**!"

"Debra, we are so proud of you," her mother said as she came into the waiting area followed by her father and grandfather.

"I am so proud of you, Debra. What an **accomplished pianist** you are becoming, my dear granddaughter!"

"Thank you, Grandpa. I'm so glad you could come." Looking around the room, she said, "I thought Mildred was going to come with you."

"She was, my dear. However, she said to give you her apologies. She came down with a migraine rather unexpectedly."

"I see," Debra replied while glancing at her mother with a knowing look. It was only a few weeks ago that she had had a confrontation with Mildred, catching her in the act of going through her personal belongings in her grandfather's old **music** room. Mildred had made it perfectly clear that she knew something suspicious was going on and that it had something to do with the **player piano**. She had further informed Debra that in no uncertain terms when she and Debra's grandfather got married, the first thing to go would be the ugly **player piano**. Debra had tried unsuccessfully to warn her grandfather, but he seemed to think Mildred was just having an off day, or it was a slight misunderstanding. She worried that Mildred had cast some type of spell over her grandfather, and being so in love, he couldn't see her true colors. She now understood the statement 'love is blind.'

Cutting into her thoughts, Debra's father asked, "Would you like to go out for some ice cream to celebrate your success tonight?"

"Yes, Dad, I would love to. Can we go to Snelgrove's?"

"Absolutely, if that's where you'd like to celebrate your success, then I'm more than happy to treat us all. Are you ready to go?"

"I'm just going to say a quick goodbye to Mrs. Hocking and I'll meet you in the car."

Ted walked in the front door, calling to his mother that he was home.

"Hello, Ted, I'm surprised to see you home on a Saturday night. You're usually working late at the Olive Garden. Is everything okay, dear?"

"Everything is great, Mom. I just needed a night off. What's for dinner?"

"I made a large pan of enchiladas. There are leftovers you can warm up in the microwave."

"That **sounds** good. Thanks, Mom." It wasn't long before he was enjoying his dinner and thinking about Debra and her **recital**. It felt good to know he had found a girl who loved **music** as much as he did and who liked to work hard to achieve her goals. He hated to see the summer come to an end because it would mean less time he would have to spend with her. She was a couple of years younger than he was and would be starting her last year of high school in a few weeks. He was in college and had just finished the summer quarter about a month ago. He normally didn't mind staying immersed with school and work, but since meeting Debra over the summer, he had to admit it was nice to have a break from school for a few weeks to squeeze in any spare time he had to spend with her.

Not only did they have crazy schedules to coordinate seeing each other, but they also lived in two different states. Debra was from

Salt Lake City, Utah and he was from Huntington Beach, California. He smiled when he remembered the day **Middle C** had picked him up at his **rest** stop, and upon entering the **music** mobile, he spotted the feisty redhead, now known to him as Debra Wilkin. He shook his head as he thought about the days when he didn't trust pretty girls and would have never intentionally let down his guard to **sing** for anyone he knew. He still had some painful memories of being teased by his peers while growing up for having such a high **voice** for a guy. Somehow Debra had worked her magic on him, and he had opened up and shared his painful past, exposing his most vulnerable secrets. With her encouragement and support, he started to **sing** again and could even admit now that he loved to **sing** and enjoyed sharing his **talent** with others. Even with all the challenges of being able to spend time together, he knew that he and Debra had been brought together for a special purpose.

"How was your dinner, Ted?" his mother asked, coming into the kitchen.

"Delicious, Mom, it totally hit the spot. Thanks for saving me some leftovers."

"I can't let my boy starve to death now, can I?"

"I guess not. Would it be okay if I use the phone to call Debra?" Ted asked. "Her **piano recital** was this afternoon, and I'd like to call her and see how it went. When the phone bill comes, I'll pay you back for the call."

"Of course you can, Ted, and thanks for offering to pay me back for your portion of the bill. It's too bad that you weren't able to attend. It must be very challenging to have your girlfriend live in another state."

"It definitely has its moments, that's for sure. The upside is I can focus on my **studies** and work without worrying about a girlfriend getting in my way, but I do miss her when I want to see her. I keep reminding myself we were brought together for a reason, and somehow, it's all going to work out. I'm not sure how, but I have faith it will."

"I have faith in you, son, and if you say it will, then I believe it will too."

"I'm going to go into the den and use the phone so I can have some privacy, okay, Mom?"

"You go ahead, dear. I'll finish up in the kitchen."

"Hello."

"Debra, is that you?"

"Hi, Ted! It's so good to hear your **voice**. Thank you so much for the roses. I loved them, and they did bring me good luck! I wish you could have been there."

"I felt like I was there, and I could imagine you **playing** every **note** perfectly."

"It's interesting that you say that because after I received your roses, for a moment I was sure I felt your presence. Isn't that weird?"

"No, it's not weird at all, Debra. Would you believe me if I told you I was there?"

"Yes, I would, especially if **Middle C** had anything to do with it. Did he by chance sprinkle some fairy dust on the two of you and you observed me as a speck of dust?"

"Something tells me **Middle C** has used some fairy dust on you. Care to enlighten me?"

"Remember a few weeks ago when **Middle C** dropped us off for an hour and we got to spend some time together? It was the day I was so upset over Mildred. When **Middle C** was flying me back to my grandfather's home, he detected Mildred going through the bag I had left by the side of the **player piano**. We couldn't let her see us land and find out about **Middle C**, so he threw some fairy dust in the air, and we were able to land as a speck of dust. I took some extra fairy dust into the downstairs bathroom with me and was able to **transpose** myself back into my normal size. Boy, did I shock her when I came out of the bathroom."

"What happened next?"

"I asked her if she found what she was looking for. I could tell I had caught her by surprise, and she told me that she knew something was going on, and she wasn't going to stop until she got to the bottom of it. She also informed me that when she and my grandfather get married, the first thing to go will be the ugly **player piano**."

"Wow, Debra, this is getting a little creepy. I hope you were able to talk to your grandfather about her."

"I tried to tell him, but he is either blinded by his love for her or she has cast some kind of spell over him. The only good thing is that **Middle C** witnessed the whole thing and reassured me that I wasn't exaggerating. He said he would try to help me figure out a plan. I'm really worried about what Mildred will do to my grandfather."

"It **sounds** like you have good reason to be worried. Did your grandfather come to your **recital**?"

"Yes, he did. He told me he would be bringing Mildred, but she didn't come, stating she had a migraine at the last minute. Imagine that! I have to admit I was relieved that she didn't come. My dad took us out for ice cream after, and it was nice to be able to enjoy the evening without having to put up with Mildred's moodiness."

"I'm glad you were able to have a good time, but I am concerned about this situation with Mildred. Maybe on Monday, before or after class, we can get together with **Middle C** to brainstorm on some ideas of how to get this situation under control. What do you think?"

"I think it's a good idea, and the sooner, the better. From what I can see, Mildred has her own agenda, and it's going to take the three of us working overtime to **ritard** whatever she has up her sleeve."

"Well, that's enough about Mildred. Let's talk about something exciting. Next weekend is the last weekend before school starts, and it's also our big week to go on our personal **music** tours to meet our **music** idols! Are you looking forward to it?"

"It's funny you should mention that. I thought a lot about that before I went out to **perform** my **recital piece** today. I kept telling myself to relax because compared to next week and **performing** for Debosney, **playing** in the **recital** would be a **piece** of cake!"

"Debra, I can't figure out why you get so nervous. You are such a **gifted pianist**, and you always **perform** at a superb level. Where does all your self-doubt come from?"

"I'm not sure, Ted. I just want to always do my best, and I don't want Debosney to be disappointed with the way I **perform** his **music**."

"I'm pretty sure you don't have to worry about that. Even **Middle C** said today after hearing you **play** at your **recital**, he was sure Debosney couldn't have **performed** any better."

"Wow, Ted, thanks for sharing that with me! From now on if I start to doubt myself, I'm going to remember what you just told me, and it'll give me the confidence I need to believe in myself. Getting back to your question about whether I'm excited…yes, I am. I'm a little nervous too because France is so far away, and I can't figure out how time will stand still while we're gone for a few days. My instructor keeps telling me not to worry—that in this **music realm** the impossible becomes possible. How are you dealing with everything?"

"I can't wait to meet Lucious Caparoni! I have so many things I want to ask him. I'm more worried about running out of time. I think it also helps to be a guy. You've probably noticed my build, and not too many guys try to mess with me due to my size. Please don't take that the wrong way, Debra, I'm not bragging. It's just a result of all my hard work."

"I happen to be a fan of your big muscles, Ted! After noticing your dazzling smile, your broad shoulders got my attention immediately!"

"Is that so, Miss Debra?" Ted said with a happy chuckle.

"Yes, Mr. Nobson, that is definitely so!"

"Well, I'm glad you find me attractive because I happen to think you're out-of-this-world gorgeous! I may get a little jealous that Debosney gets to spend time with you."

"You don't need to worry about that. I like Debosney for his **music**, but you have everything else I'm looking for in a guy."

"I like hearing that, Debra, thanks. Well, it's getting late, and I should let you get ready for bed. I'll look forward to seeing you on Monday. Sleep well."

"I'm so glad you called Ted, and thanks again for the roses. They meant so much to me. I look forward to Monday too, and hope it'll be here soon. Good night."

Chapter 2

Monday morning found Debra hurrying through her morning routine, anxious to be on her way to her grandfather's home. Packing her bag of things to take with her, she reached for the notebook she had purchased over the weekend and slipped it inside. Today her instructor, Brenda, would be going over the final details of her trip to France, and she wanted to take **notes** so she wouldn't forget anything vital. Taking a quick glance at her reflection in the hall mirror, she rushed upstairs.

"Good morning, Debra. You seem to be in a big hurry today. Is everything okay, honey?"

"Everything's great. I'm just trying to squeeze in as much time as I can with Grandpa before school starts next week. This summer went by way too fast for me!"

"Speaking of school, we need to finish up your shopping for school clothes. What have you got planned for tomorrow? Can we go then and finish up?"

"Tomorrow will be perfect. The only good thing about going back to school is getting new clothes, so I'll definitely look forward to going shopping."

"Okay, dear. Before you leave, let me get a bottle of home-made strawberry jam for you to give to Grandpa." Handing the jar to Debra, she watched as Debra walked to the front door. "You be careful, Debra, and I'll see you later this afternoon."

Blowing a kiss to her mother, she walked to her car and immediately noticed the coolness in the morning temperature. That could

mean only one thing—fall was on its way, and school would be starting soon! Before she had met Ted, she had always looked forward
to school starting and all the fun activities that came along with it.
Smiling, she could picture her group of friends and laughed when
she thought about the numerous ways they concocted to meet guys.
Now that Ted was in her life, she wasn't sure how she felt about
attending all those events anymore. It would be different if Ted could
attend the activities with her. She wondered if she could find a way
to make that happen. While backing out of the driveway, she turned
on the radio and heard a **song** that reminded her of Ted and couldn't
help **singing** along. When she arrived at her grandfather's, she was in
a great mood, despite seeing Dale mowing the lawn.

"Good morning, Grandpa," Debra said while kissing him on
the cheek as he held the door open for her.

"How's my Debra today?"

"I'm fantastic! Look what I have for you! A bottle of homemade
jam from my mom just for you! How are you doing?"

"Looks like strawberry—my favorite! I'm doing incredible now
that I have my favorite jam. Mildred's on her way over, and we'll be
going for our morning walk as soon as she arrives."

Debra tried not to show her disappointment at hearing him
mention Mildred's name. "Should I hurry downstairs and beckon
Middle C before she gets here?" Debra asked with concern in her
voice.

"That may be a good idea, Debra. I've tried to bring up the
subject of the **player piano** with Mildred, but for some reason we're
always interrupted whenever I bring up that particular subject."

"I don't believe that's just a coincidence, Grandpa. Mildred has
a definite agenda when it comes to the **player piano**. I'm not trying
to cause trouble or tell you what to do, but you really need to talk to
her about it and figure out what she plans to do. It could be a make-
or-break decision for you on whether you decide to keep Mildred in
your life."

"I'm sure you're overreacting, Debra. However, I will discuss
it with her as it very well could make a difference on any future
arrangements. For now, let's enjoy this day—you with your **music**

plans and your upcoming trip to France, and I'll handle the talk with Mildred. Run along, dear girl, before we get interrupted."

"Okay, Grandpa. I love you and only want what's best for you. Do you know that?"

"Yes, and thank you for worrying about me."

Debra reached out to give him a hug and then hurried into the kitchen to exit and make her way down to the old **music** room. Before beckoning **Middle C**, she went into the downstairs bathroom to check her appearance. She had felt a few tears slip down her cheeks while talking to her grandfather and wanted to make sure she didn't have any mascara tracks. Relieved that she still looked presentable, she rushed over to the **player piano** and quickly triggered the mechanism that brought the arrival of **Middle C**.

"Good morning, Debra! Are you looking forward to finalizing the details of your trip to meet Mr. Debosney?"

"Yes, I'm both excited and nervous. We also need to be on our way because my grandfather is expecting Mildred to drop by any minute."

"Say no more on that subject," **Middle C** responded and reached with lightning speed to pull out his **metronome** to begin setting the dials for their trip to the **conservatory**. Within seconds, the **notes** and delightful **tune** swept them up and away into the **music** mobile without leaving any trace that they had been in the old **music** room.

Debra took a seat fairly close to **Middle C**, wanting to talk to him about Mildred before they stopped to pick up Ted. "I told my grandfather that he really needed to talk to Mildred, and he said that every time he tries to bring up the subject of the **player piano**, they always seem to get interrupted."

"That's not too surprising after experiencing our little **scenario** with Mildred," **Middle C** snorted.

"I agree. In fact, Ted and I were talking over the weekend and decided that the three of us need to brainstorm and come up with a few of our own **techniques** on how to handle the problem of Mildred."

"Based on Mildred's recent **performance**, I can only conclude that the sooner we develop our own **arrangements**, the quicker our

transition from her negative **tone** will be!" Debra felt the landing of the **music** mobile and anxiously waited to see Ted.

"Good morning, **Middle C**, Debra. How are two of my favorite people on this beautiful day?" Ted asked while climbing aboard.

"Debra and I were just lamenting over the state of affairs with regard to Mildred and are anxious to get your feedback on how to **fine-tune** this situation we have found ourselves in with her."

"I've been thinking about our predicament too, and if we can figure out what her motivation is for getting rid of the **player piano**, it will help us in **transitioning** a plan to **modulate** a change in getting Mildred to start **marching** to a new **tune**, or our only other option will be to convince Debra's grandfather that he's making a grandiose mistake if he continues to see her."

"Mr. **Middle C**, do you by chance have some type of fairy dust that we could sprinkle on Mildred to **transpose** her into a nicer person?"

"An excellent suggestion, Debra. However, regrettably the answer is no. I think we are in the right **range**, and with repeated focus we will **register** the right theme for handling her. For now, it's time we were on our way to the **conservatory**, where you two have earned a trip of a lifetime, and your focus will be better served there. The problem of Mildred, I'm sure, will still be here when we return, and we can revisit that issue once our **tempo** has been refreshed."

"Paul, isn't that Debra's car parked in your driveway?" Mildred asked as she reached possessively for his hand when they set out for their walk.

"Yes, it is."

"Really, Paul, why does she have to spend so much time at your home? Don't you think it's a little bit peculiar for someone of her age to spend so much time here?"

"I enjoy having Debra spend time at my home. We both love **music**, and it thrills me to see her love for **music** growing by leaps and bounds. Which reminds me, Mildred, we need to finish our conversation about my **player piano**. Every time I try to bring up the subject, we keep getting interrupted. Debra is under the impression from a conversation you had with her, that if we were to get married, the first thing you're going to get rid of is my **player piano**. Why would you tell her something like that?"

"Paul, I have no idea where she came up with a ridiculous notion like that. Why on earth would I say something so preposterous? I can only conclude that she is jealous of the time I am spending with you and is now concocting stories to drive a wedge between us!"

"Mildred, I really have to disagree with you. Debra is not the kind of girl who would try to interfere. She is one of the sweetest granddaughters I have."

"So what are you saying, Paul? Are you insinuating that I am a liar? This conversation is the absolute proof in the pudding that Debra is trying to come between us. Mark my word, if you don't put a stop to how much time she spends at your home, you will be in for a lifetime of misery and loneliness!"

"Now, Mildred, let's not blow this conversation out of proportion. Let's get back to the original question of my **player piano**. Would you get rid of it if we were to get married?"

"I am too upset to even discuss this subject rationally right now. I can see that I'm not that important to you, Paul. As soon as we go around this next corner, I'm going straight home. I can feel a migraine coming on this very minute!"

"I certainly didn't mean to upset you, Mildred. However, I do need to know how you feel about **music** as it **plays** a very important role in my life." He studied Mildred as she gave him the **silent** treatment and then turned the corner, walking determinedly toward her home. "I'm sorry you're not feeling well, and I hope you get feeling better soon, Mildred."

Before leaving, Mildred turned abruptly to him and said, "I've told you how I feel, Paul. You're going to have to decide what and whom you want in your life. I can see that Debra is only going to cause trouble between the two of us, and if we're going to have a life together, we will have to limit the time she spends at your home. I'm going in now, and I hope you will consider the seriousness of the things we've discussed today, Paul dear."

CHRISTY WILBURN NOBELLA WEBB

He watched Mildred go inside, slamming the door behind her. Was he spending time with someone who didn't share his love of **music**? After their conversation today, he was beginning to see Mildred in a whole new light and began to wonder if he might have been a little too hasty in his decision to get so involved with her. Lost in his thoughts, he turned the corner and continued walking home.

Mildred glared at Paul from her living room window, vowing to get even with that conniving Debra! How dare she come between her and Paul and ruin all her plans for a happy future. She could see that a breakup with Paul was imminent in the near future if she didn't do something about Debra **pronto**!

Debra was stunned to hear the knock on the door giving the five-minute notice to wrap up their class time.

"Do you have any more questions for me?" Brenda asked, feeling confident that she had covered all the information Debra would need for her trip to France on Wednesday.

"I'm pretty sure I have asked everything I can think of for now, Brenda. Thank you for being so patient with me. I hope I haven't driven you crazy."

"You're going to be just fine, Debra! Don't forget to relax and enjoy your trip. As you are aware, this is a rare opportunity given only to a select few who have demonstrated their true devotion to their **music**. You are being rewarded for your dedication, so this is your time to soak in every experience you can, and more importantly enjoy it all!"

"Thank you, Brenda! You are the best instructor I could ever ask for. I can't wait to share everything with you when I get back."

"I'll be here waiting anxiously to hear every detail. Run along now so you're not late for the wrap-up details in the **conservatory**."

The **conservatory** was buzzing with excitement when she entered the room, and she could hear her fellow students eagerly sharing their travel plans with each other. Ted was already seated and talking to William; however, he waved her over to join them. **Listening** to their enthusiasm about their upcoming adventures helped build her excitement for her own trip.

"Class, I'm thrilled to hear all of the positive energy that's being generated in this room. It **sounds** like everyone is in high spirits and you're all ready for your lifetime adventures. May I be the first to congratulate each of you on a job well done and express my deepest desire for all of you to enjoy a safe and memorable trip? I look forward to your return and will be anxious to hear a report on each of your experiences. Are there any questions or concerns? It looks like all is in order, and you are excused until Wednesday morning, when I'll see you back here bright and early." Mr. Walker smiled and waved as he moved to the exit in order to shake each **student's** hand as they left the room.

The **noise level** once again increased while the **students** gathered their things and began leaving the room. "Come along, Ted and Debra, **pronto**. We have much to discuss before I drop you two off," **Middle C** announced in his normal hasty manner.

Ted grabbed Debra's hand, and they hurried to follow **Middle C** out of the room. The **musical notes** immediately swept them aboard the **music** mobile. "So, **Middle C**, what's up with the big rush?" Ted asked curiously.

"I don't know if your instructors advised you that on Wednesday, I will need to pick you up an hour earlier in order to accommodate your upcoming travel **arrangements**. I will deliver you to the **conservatory**, where the girls will be traveling with **Treble Clef** and the guys will be traveling with **Bass Clef** to your various destinations."

"I hope you're kidding, Mr. **Middle C**! In case you've forgotten, Rita and I are not on the best of terms. If I don't watch her every move, I could end up getting dumped somewhere. Are you sure you can't take me?"

"I'm sorry to disappoint you, Debra. However, the **arrangements** have been made, and there's nothing that can be done about them now. **Treble Clef** is fond of you, Debra, and I'm sure won't let anything detrimental happen to you while you're under her watchful care."

Ted could tell by the expression on Debra's face that the joy of her upcoming trip was now gone. "Come on, Debra, it won't be so bad. Buddy up with Katie, and that should keep Rita on her best behavior, not allowing her to pull any sour **notes**." He gently squeezed her hand and winked at her when she looked into his eyes.

"I will have a talk with **Treble Clef** and enlighten her on your situation with Rita so she will be alert to anything amiss in her behavior. You have worked so hard my dear, Debra. Don't let Rita ruin this once-in-a-lifetime experience for you," **Middle C** consoled.

They had arrived at Ted's **rest** stop without having an opportunity to discuss what to do about the situation with Mildred. "Well… we've had quite the morning, haven't we? I don't know who causes more trouble, Rita or Mildred," **Middle C** said with a slight chuckle. "Let's all keep working on a plan to figure out what to do about Mildred, and unfortunately, we'll have to discuss that can of worms at another time. Ted, you best be on your way. I'll see you bright and early on Wednesday morning."

Ted stood to leave and leaned over and asked Debra if she was going to be okay. Watching her nod her head in the affirmative, he gently kissed her cheek. When she turned her face to his, he lightly brushed his lips across hers, whispering sweet words of comfort.

"Okay, you two, I'll see you Wednesday, and it's going to be a fantastic time for ALL of us," Ted announced with **brio** while walking to the **music** mobile exit.

Ted's enthusiasm brought a smile to Debra. What would she ever do without him? He was the life of the party! Even in the worst of conditions, he could make her smile and laugh! She blew him a kiss and waved as they departed into a cloud of swirling **notes**.

"Everything will be all right, Debra. Focus on your **music** and don't worry about Rita or Mildred. You have earned this special trip, and I trust that all will be well while you are traveling with **Treble Clef**. It's time now for me to be off, and I look forward to seeing you bright and early on Wednesday morning!" With that, he was swooped up by a full **octave** of **notes** and delivered safely back inside the old **player piano**.

Taking a deep breath to help settle her nerves, Debra turned out the light in the **music** room and slowly went up the staircase to the kitchen. Before opening the door, she **listened** cautiously to detect Mildred or her grandfather's **voice**. Opening the kitchen door quietly, she heard her grandfather call to her from the living room.

"Come and tell me about your day, Debra. Are you ready now for your trip?"

"I think I'm as ready as I'm going to be," she replied, sighing while taking a seat next to him on the couch.

"For a girl that is scheduled to go on a trip of a lifetime, you don't appear to be very excited. What happened between this morning and now when you were happily anticipating your trip?"

"Oh, Grandpa, why do things always have to be sooo complicated! Did I ever tell you about one of the **students** named Rita?"

"I can't recall any conversations about her. What's the problem?"

"It's a long story, and the best way to sum it up is to say she wants to be Ted's girlfriend and has tried to do everything she can think of to break us up. After class today, **Middle C** informed me that **Treble Clef** will be escorting the girls to their various destinations, and the guys will be traveling with **Bass Clef**. I wouldn't put it past her to try to push me out of the **music** mobile. Putting it mildly, Grandpa, I'm scared to death to be around her!"

"Oh dear, I had no idea it was that serious. No wonder you look so glum. I suppose you have **voiced** your concerns to **Middle C**?"

"Yes, he said he would talk to **Treble Clef** so she's aware of the situation in case Rita tries anything. I just don't want to spend the whole time watching my back, worrying that Rita's going to make a move to hurt me."

"We have to trust **Middle C**'s judgment on this, Debra. He wouldn't allow you to go if he thought you would be in any danger. Be alert and stay as close to **Treble Clef** as you can and all should go well."

"I promise I will, Grandpa. I'm glad we had this chance to talk. I'm a little surprised that you're not still on your walk with Mildred. Did she come over today?"

"Yes, and on our walk, I brought up the subject of the **player piano**. I will just say that bringing up that subject caused an immediate migraine for her. We had a few words, and I have to admit Debra, it's caused me to take a second look at my possible hastiness to get so involved with Mildred. I saw her in a whole new light today, and I'm not sure I liked what I saw."

"Oh, Grandpa, I'm so sorry you had to go through that, but I am grateful that you've been able to see what I've been seeing for weeks. I'm certainly not going to tell you what to do because I know you have a lot more experience in these things than I do. I just want you to know that I love you and only want the best for you." She reached over and hugged him, planting a big kiss on his cheek. "Are you going to be okay?"

"Yes, dear, this isn't my first breakup, although it certainly did come as a surprise to me. I thought I was too old to be going through this kind of stuff!"

"Well, if there's anything I can do to help, please just say the word." She checked the time and realized she needed to be going. "I hate to leave you like this, Grandpa, but if I'm going to be ready on Wednesday, I better get going."

"You run along, and don't worry about me. I'll get this situation with Mildred nipped in the bud, as we older people say."

"Okay, Grandpa, love you!" She waved as she went out the door, worrying about him while also thinking about the challenges of her upcoming trip. She hoped she would be able to handle whatever came her way.

Chapter 3

"Debra…you need to wake up, honey. It's almost noon, and we need to go shopping for your school clothes. Are you feeling okay? You haven't slept in this long all summer, and I was beginning to worry about you."

Debra set up and leaned over to look at the time on her clock radio. "Oh my word, I had no idea it was this late. I can't believe I slept so long. I must have been more tired than I thought. I'll run in the bathroom and take a quick shower and hurry upstairs. Thanks for waking me up, Mom."

While rushing through her morning routine, she could only conclude that the added stress of imagining what Rita might do to her on her upcoming trip zapped the last bit of energy she had, causing her to oversleep. She tried not to dwell on everything she still needed to do before leaving the next day on her **music** trip and instead focused on hiding her panic as she raced upstairs.

"What would you like to eat, breakfast or lunch?" her mother asked when she walked through the doorway.

"I'm not that hungry. Would it be okay if I grab some fruit, and I can eat it while we drive to the mall?"

"You do look a little pale, dear. Are you sure you're feeling okay?"

"I'll be fine. I think I was sleeping so hard that it kind of gave me a headache, and the sooner I get moving, the better I'll feel. Thank you for not being mad at me, Mom."

"I'd never be mad at you for being too tired, Debra. I'll go and get my purse while you pick out what fruit you want."

It wasn't long before they arrived at the mall. "Where would you like to go first, Debra?"

"That's a great question, Mom. I can't believe how unprepared I am this year. I don't even know what styles are in and what I would like to get. Would it be okay if we start in the middle of the mall and work our way down to JCPenney? It'll give me a chance to look at the displays in the store windows to see what's going to be popular."

"I hate to say this, Debra, but the way you've been acting lately has me very worried. I've never known you not to be on top of what school clothes you want to buy and excited about school starting. Are you sure there isn't something bothering you that you would like to talk about?"

Her thoughts went immediately to her upcoming trip and the possible threat of Rita; however, there was no way she could tell her mother about that. She remembered the conversation she had had with her grandfather about Mildred and thought this might be a safer topic to talk about. "There is something that's been on my mind, and I don't think Grandpa would mind if I told you about it." She quickly divulged the conversation she had with her grandfather about Mildred and asked her mother what she thought about it.

"My honest opinion is, I'm glad he's seeing Mildred in a new light. It's been difficult to watch my father date someone. I'm sure Mildred has her good qualities, but lately she has been very possessive of him the last few times I've seen her with him, and I have to admit I didn't care for it. Grandpa is a grown man and can take care of himself, so I don't want you to worry and let this situation get you down. I knew there was something bothering you, and I think you'll feel better now that you've been able to get it out in the open."

"Thanks for **listening**, and you're right! I'm already feeling a lot better! Let's enjoy our shopping trip."

Several hours later, with their arms piled high with shopping bags, Debra and her mother laughed as they struggled to carry all their purchases into the house. "I don't know about you, Debra, but I could certainly use a nap after all this shopping." Her mother chuckled while placing the shopping bags on the kitchen table.

"You definitely deserve one after being such a good sport and going into almost every store in the mall. Let me know what's for dinner, and I will help out for sure!"

"I'm going to take you up on that. Let's make dinner easy tonight and have tacos. In about an hour, will you start the meat and then wake me up once you have it browned?"

"Don't you worry about a thing, Mom, except for having a restful nap. I'll wake you up when the meat is ready."

Carrying the shopping bags down to her room, she thought about her new clothes and was excited for Ted to see her looking cute and up-to-date in the latest fashions. She stacked the bags carefully into a corner of her room and hurried to her desk to pull out the list she had made earlier, reminding her of what she still needed to do to get ready for her trip. If she stayed focused and didn't panic, she could get it all done and would then be able to relax as the hours ticked by to the big day.

Dinner was delicious, and Debra was wiping the table off while telling her sisters, Sydney and Linda, about her shopping trip.

"I can't wait for you to show us your new stuff, Debra. It's nice to be about the same size, so maybe we could trade clothes now and then," Linda suggested.

"I love your taste in clothes, and I wouldn't mind trading off anytime," Debra said excitedly. She could even picture herself being almost as stylish as Rita if Linda were to let her borrow some of her clothes. Wouldn't that be fun to give Rita a little competition in the clothes department!

Returning to her bedroom, she went through her things and checked her list one more time to make certain she hadn't forgotten anything. Confident that she had everything packed and ready, she pulled the shopping bags out of the corner of her room, hung up her new clothes, and then went upstairs to **practice** her **song** several more times, ensuring it would be as perfect as possible for her upcoming **performance** for Mr. Debosney.

Debra was wide awake before her alarm clock even **sounded**, not wanting to repeat what happened the day before of oversleeping, and, thankfully her nerves cooperated, only allowing her to sleep lightly. Wanting to look her best, she washed her hair and once it was styled, decided it was one of her best hair days! She looked heavenward and thanked whomever was in charge for the great hair day and prayed her day would continue to go as smoothly! Picking up her bag, she hoped her mother wouldn't notice how overpacked it was today and quietly rushed upstairs. When she arrived in the kitchen, the light was on; however, she could hear her parents talking down the hall in their bedroom. With luck on her side, she quickly went outside and placed her bag on the backseat of the car and was able to slip back inside the kitchen, **beating** her mother there. Noticing that the fruit still needed to be sliced, she began working on it, hoping to surprise and divert her mother's attention with her good deed.

"Oh look, I have a little elf working away in my kitchen this morning," her mother said when she entered the room. "Good grief, Debra, after your sleep-in yesterday, I certainly didn't expect to see you before noon today."

"I decided I couldn't sleep my last few summer vacation days away, so I thought I'd get an early start and go over and visit Grandpa today."

"I'm sure he'll enjoy that. You are a very thoughtful granddaughter."

Debra sighed inwardly with relief that everything was moving along smoother than she had anticipated and considered it a good sign for the day. Giving her mother an extra hug goodbye, she dashed to the car, wanting to be on her way. After saying a quick prayer, she turned on the radio and **sang** all the way to her grandfather's house to help keep her nerves under control. His home looked a little dark when she pulled up, and she wondered if he was awake. Grabbing her bag from the backseat, she hurried up the stairs and knocked on his door. It wasn't long before the porch light came on and he opened the door for her to enter.

"Good morning, Debra. You look beautiful and ready for your trip. Is all well with you this morning?"

"So far, so good, Grandpa. Thanks for asking. I hope I'm not too early for you."

"Any time is the right time for a visit from you, Debra. I suspect **Middle C** is anxious to go and has scheduled an early departure?"

"You know **Middle C** very well. He told us we needed to leave an hour earlier than normal."

"Well, in that case, I won't hold you up. However, I will need a hug before I let you go."

"Gladly, Grandpa," she said as she hugged him extra tight.

"There, there, my dear, you're going to be all right and will most likely have a trip you'll never forget! I'll be waiting anxiously to hear all the details about your fabulous visit with Mr. Debosney."

"I love you, Grandpa."

"And I love you too, Debra. Make me proud."

"I'll do my best."

"I know you will. You better be on your way now, my dear."

She waved lovingly at him and turned to go downstairs. All the memories of the past few months seemed to flood through her mind as she continued down to the old **music** room. It all seemed so familiar but yet so strangely different today. Even the squeaky door moaned a little **louder**. Placing her bag gently by the **player piano**, she sped into the bathroom to check her appearance. Seeing all was well, she took a deep breath to calm her nerves once more and then carefully approached the **player piano** where she beckoned **Middle C**. The familiar **notes** seemed aware that something was in the air, and they too **sounded** slightly different, making her wonder if it was a good idea for her to go on this trip.

Startling her, **Middle C** asked, "Are you ready for your **music** adventure, Debra?"

"Yeees, I think so, Mr. **Middle C**. Well, as ready as I'll ever be, that is."

"That's the spirit, dear girl," he replied cheerfully while reaching into his tuxedo to remove his trusty **metronome**. Soon the **notes** began an intricate dance, twisting and turning in all directions while she gathered up her bag and then just as quickly depositing them onto the **music** mobile, leaving the **music** room behind in the twinkling of an eye.

Debra stared out the side of the **music** mobile, lost in thought, while she waited for **Middle C** to arrive at Ted's **rest** stop. Normally it didn't take long to arrive at Ted's **rest** stop, so when their journey seemed longer than usual, she questioned **Middle C** on why it was taking so long to reach Ted.

"There was a last-minute change in plans due to a conflict in scheduling with **Bass Clef**. He will be picking up Ted, whereas we will be going directly to the **conservatory**, where we will meet **Treble Clef** and the other two **students**. I'm sorry to be the bearer of bad news, Debra, but it couldn't be helped."

"So will I get to see Ted at all today?"

"As far as I know, **Bass Clef** will be delivering him straight to his chosen destination. I know this is not what you wanted to hear, Debra, and I hope that it won't take away from the pleasure of your visit to see Mr. Debosney. I assure you, Mr. Debosney has heard about your love of his **music** and can't wait to meet you."

"I admit, I was hoping to see Ted before leaving on my trip, but things do change that can't be helped at the last minute. I appreciate your telling me about Mr. Debosney looking forward to my visit. At this point, the best thing for me to do is not feel sorry for myself but instead focus all my energy into my meeting with Mr. Debosney."

"I agree, Debra, and we'll be arriving shortly at the **conservatory**."

Things were bustling at the **conservatory** when they arrived, and Debra noticed a larger version of a **music** mobile sitting in the parking lot and assumed it would be what she would travel in with **Treble Clef**.

"Come along, Debra, let's see what **arrangements** have been made for you."

She nervously followed **Middle C** while keeping a cautious eye out for Rita. While walking down the hallway to their normal meeting room at the **conservatory**, she could hear several conversations going on at the same time, but above all, there was one very distinct **high-pitched voice**, which she recognized immediately as **Treble Clef**'s.

"Awww…here is **Middle C** at last with our final passenger, Debra." Taking a quick look at her watch, she continued, "Nice of you to join us, **Middle C**, and not a minute too soon. We have a very tight schedule to meet, and we must depart at once," she replied curtly while **tapping** her foot to a strict **syncopated rhythm**.

Debra looked at Katie and then Rita and didn't miss seeing the impatient roll of Rita's eyes at having to wait an extra second for her. Determined not to let Rita get the **upbeat** on her, she **marched** over to **Treble Clef** for directions, not wanting to cause any further delays. Her quick thinking appeased **Treble Clef**, and immediately any ill feelings were forgotten.

"Okay, young ladies, it's time we board our **music** mobile," **Treble Clef** announced with authority as she waved a delicate **baton** back and forth, which instantly provided a pathway of **notes** carrying them to their vehicle. Not hesitating, Debra stepped onto the trail of **notes** first and was grateful she kept her balance, not wanting to cause any further attention or embarrassment to herself. She chose a seat up front where she could be close to **Treble Clef** and before leaving, turned to look out the open side of the **music** mobile to catch a final glimpse of **Middle C**. She could feel her heart **beating** with an erratic **pulse**, and when she met **Middle C**'s eyes, she thought for sure she was going to lose it and begin to cry. He sensed her emotions and quickly gave her one of his encouraging smiles while waving enthusiastically as they flew up and away from the **conservatory**.

Debra was lost in her thoughts when **Treble Clef's high-pitched voice** interrupted them. "Sit back and relax, ladies. We will be traveling for several hours, which is pretty amazing when you stop to consider the distance we will be covering. Normally a trip in an airplane flying over the same distance would take a day's time, where we will be there in just a couple of hours. If you get chilly, there is a blanket conveniently located under each seat for your traveling comfort. When we arrive, we will be checking into a luxurious hotel, where you can **rest** and have a meal before continuing on to your final destinations."

Debra had to admit that traveling in the **music** mobile was quite a luxury, and she wouldn't miss having to sit for endless hours flying on an airplane. She looked back and took **note** of where Katie and Rita were sitting and felt thrilled when Katie smiled and waved back at her. She couldn't help wishing that Rita would be that nice. Soon, her mind drifted off to thoughts of Ted, wondering how his adventure was going.

Rita sat smugly in her seat staring at Debra while thinking about an interesting encounter she had had with a most unusual lady named Mildred. She was under the impression that no one disliked Debra as much as she did—that was until she met Mildred. Rita had worked hard to discover where Debra's **transition** point was located and precisely how **Middle C** transported her to the **conservatory**. After careful pleading and begging, she had convinced her **music mediator**, **Largo**, to confide in her that he had heard Debra used an old **player piano** in her grandfather's basement.

She smiled when she thought about her persuasive **skills** of influencing **Largo** into dropping her off in the neighborhood where Debra's grandfather's home was located under the guise of comparing **notes** on how to prepare for their upcoming tours. While making her way to his home, she actually bumped into Mildred, who was apparently having a bad day. She had made the unpardonable mistake of mentioning Debra's name and asking if she knew her and where her grandfather lived. If words could kill, she would have been dead on the spot as disgust and loathing were instantly apparent in Mildred's demeanor. Being the cunning and master manipulator she was, she soon had Mildred **singing** an **aria** on how she had become a victim to Debra's **masterpiece** of rejection by her grandfather. After careful consoling, she soon put the **pieces** together and now working as a **duet**, they were coming up with their own clever **compositions** on how to handle the problem of Debra. If Debra only knew what her future held for her, she wouldn't be sitting so comfortable and unconcerned right now. Rita couldn't wait for the fireworks to begin!

Debra walked into her hotel room and placed her suitcase on the bed, relieved she had arrived safely on her flight from the **conservatory**. **Treble Clef** had booked a room across the hall from her and had placed Rita and Katie in rooms on a wing several floors above theirs. The bed looked comfortable, and Debra was looking forward to getting some sleep before continuing on to France. Pulling her nightgown over her head, she marveled at the delicious dinner she had just enjoyed in the company of **Treble Clef**, Katie, and Rita. The conversation had been stimulating, and Rita was actually delightful to be around, which made her feel all the guiltier for wondering what her ulterior motives were. She wanted to like and trust Rita; however, her past behavior had been less than trustworthy. Debra finished getting ready for bed and soon began to fall asleep happy in the knowledge that Rita wouldn't be traveling in the same direction as she would in the morning.

Chapter 4

Debra awoke to the **ringing** of the alarm clock that **rest**ed on the nightstand beside her bed. Not expecting to sleep very well, she was grateful she had set the alarm. Pushing the covers aside, she slid out of bed to begin her day, not wanting to be late. While getting dressed, her thoughts were immediately about her family, wondering what they were doing and if they even missed her. She would never understand how time kept moving forward where she was but stood still where her family was. For all intents and purposes, they were totally clueless about where she was and what she was doing, which made her feel slightly guilty for being so far away without her parents' knowledge; however, her grandfather knew where she was and that seemed to justify her actions for now.

She had packed a dress to wear for her meeting with Mr. Debosney, wanting to make a good first impression. After seeing how wrinkled it had gotten from being stuffed in her bag, she was relieved to see that the hotel had an ironing board and iron, and she hurriedly pulled it out of the closet so she could iron it while waiting for the hot rollers in her hair to dry. She put the finishing touches on her makeup and hair, slipped on her dress, and then took a final look in the mirror at her reflection when she remembered she would be flying to Paris, France, today and wondered for the umpteenth time how she would be able to communicate when she couldn't speak a word of French. Remembering Brenda's advice "not to worry, the impossible became possible in the **realm** of **music**," she walked out of the hotel room and made her way to the dining area.

It wasn't difficult to find the dining room, she simply followed her nose to the wonderful smells of bacon and eggs, pancakes, and waffles hot off the grill, and did she mention freshly baked cinnamon rolls and fresh fruit? A girl could certainly get used to this **music realm** in a heartbeat!

"Good morning, Debra. I trust you slept well?" **Treble Clef** inquired in her **high-pitched soprano voice**.

"I slept surprisingly well. How did you sleep, **Treble Clef**?"

"On the whole, I slept astonishingly well myself, in spite of being away from my **staff**, which I'm not accustomed to. Be that as it may, it would behoove us to eat our breakfast in an **allegro** fashion so we can **transition** as soon as possible."

Debra watched in awe as **Treble Clef marched** through the all-you-can-eat buffet line while taking one of everything. How she ever managed to maintain her slim shape was beyond her! She, on the other hand, wasn't a big breakfast eater, so her plate consisted mainly of fresh cut watermelon, cantaloupe, and pineapple, along with a cinnamon roll drenched in frosting and melted butter, which was too irresistible to pass up. Looking around the room, she saw that **Treble Clef** had joined the table where Katie and Rita were sitting, and not wanting to be standoffish, she made her way to their table.

"Well, you can certainly tell that Debra doesn't care if she gains weight," Rita commented with disgust when Debra sat down with her breakfast plate.

Deciding to keep **harmony**, she ignored Rita's comment acting as if it never **registered** her **hearing range**. Rita was about to make another comment when Debra saw **Treble Clef** give her a look that could have **silenced** cheerleaders at a victory rally.

Not missing a **beat**, **Treble Clef** interrupted the prolonged **silence** by stating, "Let's plan on meeting at the **music** mobile in forty-five minutes, which should give each of you plenty of time to finish your breakfast, collect your personal items from your rooms, while I'm settling our hotel bill. Can I count on each of you to do your part?"

They all nodded their heads in agreement, not wishing to invoke **Treble Clef**'s wrath on any of them. Debra debated about eating her cinnamon roll, especially after Rita's rude comment and decided it would be worth every mouthwatering bite to annoy Rita as she savored her pastry.

Everyone was on time and waiting to board the **music** mobile when **Treble Clef** arrived. Debra had waited inside the hotel until **Treble Clef** had concluded her business, not wanting to take a chance on getting into a confrontation with Rita. Once settled inside the **music** mobile, **Treble Clef** handed each student a small box, advising, "Inside you will find a very useful tool. I'm sure most of you have seen or used one of these, but what I am giving you today is a priceless gift and will be the **key** to unlock your language barrier wherever you might have occasion to travel. Please keep this in a safe and secure spot as you will not want to be without it, finding it most useful and valuable. To the general public, it is called a **pitch pipe**, and it provides the **pitch** so **vocalists** have a starting **note** to begin their **performance** on **key** when a **piano** or other **instrument** is not available to **tune** with. Your **pitch pipe** is similar. However, it is much more valuable because it provides a translation of whatever language you are trying to communicate in. Here's a brief example of how it works: Before you begin communicating with someone in another language, you simply blow into your **pitch pipe** three times, and it will automatically detect the language you want to communicate in. Within five seconds you will be able to continue speaking in English. However, those with whom you are speaking will hear your words in their own language. When your session or meeting has concluded, simply blow into your **pitch pipe** again three times, and it will automatically turn it off. Do you have any questions about how this **instrument** works?"

Everyone sat in awe over the explanation about how the **pitch pipe** worked, and no one had any questions; they just wanted to study their new tool. Soon, the **music** mobile was buzzing with excited chatter as the three students talked enthusiastically about their **pitch pipes**. "Thank you, **Treble Clef**, for this wonderful gift, and I will be sure to keep it safe and secure," Debra said gratefully.

Rita glared at Debra, thinking maliciously of how to steal her **pitch pipe**, which would leave her totally helpless to communicate while being stranded in Paris. Her thoughts were quickly interrupted when she heard **Treble Clef** tell Debra to prepare for their landing. Paris was their next stop. She realized there wasn't enough time to create a distraction that would be sufficient to accomplish stealing the **pitch pipe**; however, there was plenty of time to plot something for the next time. "Just count yourself lucky this time, Debra. Next time you may not be so lucky," Rita mumbled to herself.

Treble Clef got off the **music** mobile with Debra and quickly told her to use her **pitch pipe** when she saw a handsome man approaching them. Debra followed the **instructions**, praying it would work, and within just a few seconds, **Treble Clef** was introducing her to Mr. Clyde Debosney, and she could understand everything that was being said! This was absolutely amazing! A true miracle if she ever saw one!

"It is so nice to meet you, Mr. Debosney. I am in love with your **music** and can't wait to hear you **play** the **piano**. Thank you so much for agreeing to meet with me," Debra replied humbly.

"The pleasure is all mine, mademoiselle. May I also compliment you on your superb command of the French language, very impressive! I can barely denote an **accent**! I must congratulate you on your studies. Do you have everything you need so we can be off?"

Debra turned to **Treble Clef**, who nodded her head giving permission for her to accompany Mr. Debosney. "Debra, I will meet you and Clyde back here by five o'clock **sharp**. Is that agreeable to both of you?"

"Yes, **Treble Clef**, that should give us ample time to enjoy the day together, and we will be back by five o'clock **sharp**," Mr. Debosney stated while **synchronizing** his watch to **Treble Clef's**. "Now, young lady, shall we be off to the **conservatory**? As we make our way there, tell me what questions you have for me."

Debra suddenly remembered the first time she met **Middle C** and Ted and how it had sent her into a state of astonishment, freezing up her **voice** for several seconds. Once again, she could feel her throat constricting, and she was terrified she wasn't going to be able to talk despite having a **pitch pipe**. Breathing deeply to gain control over her nerves, she began to relax, and soon a calming effect took ahold of her, and she knew she was going to be okay. Turning her focus to the beautiful scenery surrounding her, she noticed Mr. Debosney studying her, and it thrilled her to realize that a wish had become a reality, and she actually was going to have the honor of spending several hours in the presence of this amazingly **talented musician**!

Clearing her throat, she began, "Mr. Debosney, I hope you will forgive my nervousness, but it is not every day a girl like me has the privilege of spending time with an admired **maestro**. Would you begin by telling me how you got started **playing** the **piano**?"

"Thank you, Debra, for your kind words. I began to take **piano lessons** when I was seven years old. I am the oldest of five children and came from a very poor family. My aunt heard me **play** when I was young and told my mother I had **talent** and she should enroll me in lessons. She believed in my **talent** so much that she even paid for my lessons. I loved taking the **lessons**, and by the age of ten, I was accepted to the Paris **conservatory**, where I spent eleven years studying there. We are on our way now to the **conservatory** so you can see firsthand where it all started."

"I am very excited to see where your **training** took place. I'm also enjoying our walk to the **conservatory**. The scenery here is breathtaking. I love walking along this pathway where the grass and trees are so green and beautifully manicured. The buildings in the background are massive and decorated so elaborately with cutout details carved to perfection. You must have enjoyed growing up in Paris, Mr. Debosney."

"Sometimes when you grow up surrounded by these structures, it's easy to take things for granted, Debra. I appreciate your pointing them out to me, so I can reassess their beauty as well. We have arrived at the **conservatory** now. Let me get the door, and we'll go inside and have a look around."

After going inside, Debra waited for Mr. Debosney to lead the way. She felt like she needed to pinch herself to see if this was really happening. They walked down several halls and entered an enormous room that contained six **baby grand pianos**, along with other **instruments** and **accompanying music paraphernalia**.

"Welcome to the Paris **conservatory**, Debra. Please take a look around and feel free to try one of these **pianos** that meets your heart's desire."

Forgetting her nervousness, and following her excitement, Debra sat down and immediately **played** through several warm-up exercises Brenda had taught her, which did wonders to loosen up the tightness in her fingers. She felt relaxed and happy and couldn't wait to **play** for him. Noticing she had his full attention, she stood and announced, "Mr. Debosney, it is my great pleasure to be able to spend this precious time with you, and I am pleased now to **perform** for you 'Clarese le Dune.'"

She seated herself once again at the **baby grand piano**, took a deep breath, and slowly began the lovely captivating **song** that had become an integral part of her life for the past several months. Her mind remembered each delicate **note** while her fingers worked meticulously to incorporate each **dynamic**, hoping to **produce** the enchanting work of art he had originally created. When she came to the final **runs**, the **song** became even more spellbinding and riveting, and the final **notes** were delivered with certainty and confidence, leaving a lasting impression that would never be forgotten by her, and certainly not by him!

"**Bravo**, dear Debra! Your **performance** was absolutely superb! You have almost left me speechless! To be truthful, dear girl, I don't know if I could **perform** 'Clarese le Dune' as **perfect**ly as you just did. Well done indeed! Please, whatever you do, don't ask me to **play** that **song** for you because I don't think I could do it the justice you just did! I will never forget the way you **performed** it, and I thank you from the bottom of my heart for making it come alive for me."

Mr. Debosney turned to look at Debra and saw that she had tears streaming down her cheeks. "Oh dear, please tell me I haven't said or done something to upset you, Debra. I assure you that was not my intention at all."

Debra swiped at the tears that continued to roll down her cheeks and fought to get control of her emotions. After a few moments, she replied, "I am not upset, Mr. Debosney, quite the contrary. I think this is perhaps one of the happiest days of my life. For the last few months, I have worked day and night to **perfect** your lovely **masterpiece**. I have daydreamed about **playing** for you, worried about **playing** for you, and now that it's happened, I am indescribably happy that I pleased you. That was my ultimate goal, to bring you joy, not dread. Thank you for your kind words of praise. I'll never forget this moment! I am looking forward to hearing you **play** and would be interested in having you tell me anything else about your **musical career** that you would like to share."

"I would be happy to do that Debra. When I was twenty-two years old, I won the **Prix de Rome**, which is a French scholarship for arts students. I felt extremely fortunate because it helped me to finance two more years of **musical study** in Italy, which was most beneficial."

Debra watched Mr. Debosney walk to the **baby grand piano** next to hers, and he described that there were a couple of **songs** he would like to **play** that he thought she would particularly enjoy. She sat mesmerized by his **talent** and **listened** with fascination at the beauty and **quality** of each **note** he drew out of the **piano**. When he was finished, she rose to give him a **standing ovation**.

"There are no words to describe your commanding presence at the **piano**, Mr. Debosney. I hope you will write down the names of the **songs** you just **performed** because I would like to purchase the **music** so I can begin **learning** them."

After writing the names of the **pieces** down, Mr. Debosney asked Debra, "Tell me what you enjoy most about my **music**…I would like to know."

"Each of your **pieces** has a sentimental and romantic quality to it. Whenever I am **playing** your **music**, I can do my best thinking. It makes me wonder about your personal life and what you have gone through in order to write such passionate **music**."

"Well, Miss Debra, you are most insightful, and I daresay you carry tender and passionate feelings inside your heart as well, which I wish we had time to go in to." He checked his watch and sighed. "I have enjoyed our time today so much and can't believe it is already time for us to go back and meet **Treble Clef**. It is my sincere hope that you will be able to schedule another visit to the **conservatory**, where we can share our love of **music** again. I would enjoy hearing you **perform** another one of my **pieces**. You definitely have a **talent** for bringing my **music** to life, and I would be most happy to be a captive **audience** to one of your **performances** again."

Debra climbed into the **music** mobile and was happy to see that the bus was empty, which meant she would have first pick on where she wanted to sit. Choosing the seat closest to where **Treble Clef** would be sitting, she sat down and remembered she still needed to turn off her **pitch pipe**. Pulling it out of its box, she blew three times into it, waited five seconds, and then returned the **pitch pipe** carefully to its box. Looking out the side of the **music** mobile, she could see **Treble Clef** talking to Mr. Debosney, and as she **listened** to their conversation in French, she found it remarkable that only a few seconds ago, she could understand every word being spoken, whereas now it **sounded** completely foreign to her. The **music realm** was certainly filled with all kinds of mysteries, and she wondered if she would ever understand how it all worked. She thought about her grandfather and decided this was a subject she wanted to discuss with him to **learn** if he had solved any of its mysteries. She felt the **music** mobile **rock** and looked up in time to see **Treble Clef** looking directly at her.

"You are to be congratulated, Debra, on an outstanding visit with Mr. Debosney. He informed me that you **performed** 'Clarese le Dune' better than anyone else he has ever heard. That is extremely high praise, young lady, and I know from experience that Mr. Debosney does not give **compliments** lightly."

"Thank you, **Treble Clef**. I will cherish the memories I made today with Mr. Debosney, and am so grateful to have had this experience. Have you had a good day?"

"I have enjoyed my day as well. However, I won't mind getting back to my **staff** and my normal routine. If you have everything, let's be off."

Debra watched as **Treble Clef** reached into a satchel and pulled out a very attractive **baton**, which she began to **wave**, picking up the **tempo** as more and more **notes** made their **debut**. Once they were airborne and Debra sensed that **Treble Clef** was more relaxed, she asked, "After you pick up Katie and Rita, will we make it back tonight to our **conservatory**?"

"Yes, Debra, that is what I am planning to do at this moment as long as we don't encounter any unplanned interruptions."

It seemed like days, instead of hours, by the time they landed at the **conservatory**. Debra noticed that Katie looked like she had had an enjoyable day; however, Rita looked like a storm cloud ready to erupt at any moment. Deciding it best to mind her own business, she avoided eye contact with her, not wanting to **fiddle** or create any sour **notes**. When Rita had left the **music** mobile, she followed Katie out, all the while looking for Ted and **Middle C**.

"Welcome back, Debra! How was your trip to see Mr. Debosney?" **Middle C** asked, moving with **brio** in her direction.

"I had the best day I could have ever hoped for, Mr. **Middle C**! Mr. Debosney is truly a **maestro** at the **piano** and was so kind and patient with me," she responded happily.

"Debra is also being very modest about her visit, and more importantly, her **performance** of 'Clarese le Dune,'" **Treble Clef** informed **Middle C**. "Clyde told me himself that he had never heard anyone else **perform** his **masterpiece** as well as our Debra!"

"Oh, Debra, no wonder you are glowing with delight! Clyde does not hand out compliments lightly, so you must have **performed** incredibly."

"Weren't those my exact words, Miss Debra?" **Treble Clef** asked emphatically.

"You two certainly know Mr. Debosney well," Debra replied with a chuckle.

"Thank you for taking good care of Debra, and now, dear girl, shall we get you back home?" **Middle C** asked.

"Yes, Mr. **Middle C**," Debra replied while continuing to look around for Ted.

Noticing Debra's search for Ted, **Middle C** replied, "Once again, I'm afraid you're going to be disappointed, Debra. **Bass Clef** delivered Ted's group back a few hours earlier. By now he's most likely home and in bed asleep."

"I was hoping I would see him so we could catch up on things. I'm pretty tired myself, so it's probably best that we just get me back to my grandfather's house so I can get home too."

Debra caught herself nodding several times on her flight back to her grandfather's. Saying a quick goodbye to **Middle C**, she picked up her bag and carried it upstairs to the kitchen, where her grandfather was waiting for her.

"Welcome back, Debra. I'm so happy to see you. How was your trip?"

"It was incredible, Grandpa! Mr. Debosney said he had never heard anyone **play** his **song** like I did, and he begged me not to ask him to **play** it because he didn't think he could do it justice like I had! Can you believe that?"

"Yes, dear girl, I can. You underestimate your talent and ability! I can see that you're exhausted, so let's pick up this conversation again in a day or so. Are you okay to drive yourself home?"

"Yes…I just hope I can stay awake once I get there."

"Well, I'll call your mother and tell her I had you do a couple of projects for me and you're dead tired and could use a good night's sleep as soon as possible. Will that work?"

"You're the best, Grandpa. I don't know what I'd do without you! Thanks for all you do. I'm going to go now, but I promise to fill you in on more details once I'm **rest**ed."

As Debra backed out of the driveway, Mildred ducked behind a big tree across the street from her grandfather's house, not wanting Paul or Debra to catch her spying on them. It infuriated her to see Debra's car there once again, spending hours over at his home. Why couldn't she be a normal teenager and hang out with other teenagers doing what teenagers do? Her only saving grace at this point was remembering the other day when she had run into Rita, who disliked her as much as she did. If only she would get back into town so they could put their heads together to figure out what to do about the problem of Debra! After waiting several more minutes until she was sure Debra was gone and Paul wouldn't catch her outside his home, she walked back the way she had come.

Chapter 5

D ebra woke up feeling **rest**ed and quickly sat up, lifting her arms up to the ceiling so she could stretch all her muscles. Her mind immediately went to thoughts of her recent adventure, and for a second, she wondered if it had all been a dream or if it had really taken place. Bending over and reaching for her purse, she had a quick way of verifying the truth. Rummaging through her purse, she soon found what she was looking for and pulled the incredible box out that contained her magical **pitch pipe**. Lifting it out carefully from its box, she reverently inspected it, remembering in awe its ability to discern whatever language she exposed it to. Smiling, she recalled Mr. Debosney's compliment about how well she had studied and mastered the French language, resulting in him barely detecting her French accent. Placing the **pitch pipe** tenderly back inside its box, she decided to keep it in a locked drawer of her desk for safekeeping.

While debating about what to wear, she heard her mother coming down the stairs. "Good morning, sleepyhead. I was beginning to worry about you, Debra, It's not like you to sleep so long. Are you feeling okay?"

"Good morning, Mom, or should I say good afternoon? I am doing great, just taking advantage of my last week of freedom before school starts next week, and I have to get up early!"

"Well…as long as that's all it is, I will stop worrying about you. What are your plans for today?"

"To tell you the truth, I haven't thought that far ahead. I'm still trying to figure out what I'm going to wear," Debra said, laughing.

"Okay, dear…well, you figure that out and then come up and get something to eat. I'm going to run to the grocery store but wanted to check on you before I left."

"Thanks, Mom. As far as what my plans are, I think I'll just hang around the house and get my school things ready for next week. Is there anything you want me to do?"

"I'd love it if you would clean up the kitchen after you've finished eating, and then you can just putter around the **rest** of the day. How does that **sound**?"

"It **sounds** wonderful. Thanks, Mom." Debra was actually grateful for a day to relax and not have to rush off to the **conservatory**. As much as she wanted to see Ted, she could really use a day to just unwind and take it easy. She was sure it was just a **classic** case of jet lag, but in her case, it was a case of **music** mobile lag, if there was such a thing! While debating about what to wear, she thought about how she had been off to France for at least a day, and her mother's only worry about her was that she had slept in that morning. She would be a basket case if she really knew what she had been up to!

Ted was also struggling with a case of **music** mobile lag and would have loved to sleep for a few more hours; however, with school starting soon, he needed to finish his work at the junior high, cleaning the floors and **arranging** the classrooms with desks and chairs so everything would be in order and ready for the first day of school.

"Good morning, Ted," his mother greeted him while placing a plate of hot pancakes, bacon, and eggs in front of him.

"Morning, Mom," Ted replied as he poured the maple syrup over his pancakes and grabbed for a slice of bacon.

"What's on your agenda for the day, dear?"

"As soon as I'm finished here, I need to go over to the junior high and get things ready for school, which starts next week."

"It's hard to believe the summer's over and school's starting again, isn't it? Where does the time go?" his mother asked with a sigh.

Ted nodded in agreement and was soon lost in thought, thinking about the first part of the summer when he had met Debra, which now seemed like ages ago. He yearned to spend time with her and wondered how her trip had gone. Missing her like crazy, he hated that they hadn't been able to see or talk to each other before leaving and returning on their individual **music** tours. Tomorrow couldn't come soon enough for him, and his heart began racing when he thought about seeing her!

"**Largo**, I don't have all day for you to make up your mind!" Rita snapped at the large, wide man who was her **music mediator**, and consequently like his name, moved to his own **rhythm**, which was too **slow** to suit her! "Either you're going to help me and drop me off near Debra's grandfather's home, or you're not going to help me. I need an answer **pronto** so I can make other **arrangements** if you're not going to cooperate."

"Miss Rita, what you're requesting is highly irregular, and it doesn't make sense to me why you can't just wait until tomorrow to speak with Debra at the **conservatory**. I can lose my **position** on the **music staff** if they can't count on me to follow the **music scores**."

"**Largo**, I wouldn't ask you to do anything that would jeopardize your **position** on the **music staff!** What kind of a girl do you think I am? There wasn't time to talk to Debra once we landed at the **conservatory** yesterday, and I need to talk to her before class tomorrow. Won't you just do this one little thing for me? You can even **accompany** me if you think I'm trying to break any **rules**."

"Well, when you put it in that **tone**, I guess I can make an exception this one time, but I will be back for you in two hours **sharp**! Don't keep me waiting, Rita!"

"Ohhh, thank you, **Largo**! I promise you won't be sorry, and I'll be back in two hours **sharp**!" Rita sighed inwardly with relief, almost at her wit's end. She just had to meet with Mildred today so they could get their plan underway on how to handle the problem of Debra!

Debra had just finished cleaning up the kitchen and walked into the living room still feeling tired. Remembering she was a day ahead of her family, it finally made sense why she kept yawning. She had already lived Thursday, spending the day with Clyde Debosney, but time had stood still for her family, and here she was repeating the day a second time! No wonder she was tired! She looked forward to going to the **conservatory** tomorrow to see if everyone else was experiencing the same thing she was.

Mildred grinned like a Cheshire cat after her meeting with Rita. They were two birds of a feather that was for sure, each enjoying every minute of their plotting to get even with unsuspecting Debra. Her days were numbered, and the only thing better would be if those numbers could be **counted** on one hand. Unfortunately what they had in mind would take a little more planning to pull it off successfully. Be that as it may, the **duo** were determined, and each had their part to **play**.

Friday morning arrived, and Debra woke up refreshed, finally feeling like she had caught up on her sleep. Rushing through her morning routine, she planned to go over to her grandfather's earlier than usual so they could talk and she could tell him about her magnificent day with Clyde Debosney. She was surprised to see Dale mowing the yard when she arrived; however, he didn't seem to notice her, and she wasn't going to do anything to divert his attention.

"Good morning, Debra! Come in, it's good to see you! I'm so glad you came early so we can talk before you have to leave for the **conservatory**. Have a seat and tell me everything. I'm all **ears**."

Debra kept her grandfather spellbound while she shared every exciting detail of her trip. "Grandfather, did you get a magical **pitch pipe** when you traveled?"

"Yes, I did! Aren't they the most amazing tool ever? You know how guys love their tools in their garages? Well, I have to admit this is the best tool I've ever received or even purchased for myself. Whenever I travel, I make sure it is safely tucked into one of my pockets so I can communicate. The people I travel with think I'm a genius when it comes to speaking any language, and they **count** on me to be their interpreter. I feel a little guilty sometimes when they give me credit for speaking multiple languages, but I can't explain how I do it. Who would ever believe it, right, dear Debra?"

"You're right, Grandpa! No one would ever believe our **music** adventures!"

"Well, Debra, I am very happy for the wonderful day you had with Mr. Debosney, and it doesn't surprise me in the least that he loved your rendition of his 'Clarese le Dune.' The day I heard you **play** it, I knew you had an incredible **talent!**"

"He **played** several more **pieces** that he thought I would love, and I can't wait to begin **learning** them. Grandpa, there's something I've been wanting to ask you."

"What's that, my dear?"

"Will I ever understand the **music realm** and all of its mysteries?"

"That is a very difficult question to answer. I'm a lot older than you, and I still don't understand it all. In a way, that's the beauty of it, and what makes it so worthwhile and enticing, wouldn't you agree?"

"I never really looked at it that way. When you put it like that, I guess you wouldn't want to know everything because then it wouldn't be exciting anymore, and you wouldn't have anything to look forward to."

"That's right, Debra." The grandfather clock in the hallway began its hourly **chime**, and they both knew it was time for her to summon **Middle C**. "Well, it's about time you were on your way, dear girl. Don't forget to say hello to **Middle C** for me. I'll look forward to seeing you when you get back."

She gave her grandfather a big hug and then hurried downstairs. It wasn't long before she and **Middle C** were on their way to pick up Ted. "I imagine you and Theodore have a lot to discuss today. I will try to **direct** our **movement** into a **moderato** speed in order to give you ample time to catchup."

"Mr. **Middle C**, you are always so kind and thoughtful, and we are very lucky to have you for our **music mediator**. Thanks so much."

"My pleasure, Debra. I see Theodore now. Prepare for our **rest** stop."

Debra's heartbeat raced with pure joy as she thought about seeing Ted. If she wasn't careful, she thought for sure she would faint

CHRISTY WILBURN NOBELLA WEBB

from excitement when she felt the rocking **movement** as he boarded the **music** mobile.

"It sure is good to see you two," Ted greeted as he entered their presence. Looking ahead to see Debra, he rewarded her with one of his irresistible smiles.

"How's my lady?" he asked tenderly while taking a seat next to her.

"I am so happy to see you, Ted! I've missed you so much, and I can't wait to hear about your trip!"

"Well, that makes two of us! I'm just relieved that you don't look the worse for wear from your trip. Did Rita behave herself?"

"Yes, not because she wanted to, but because **Middle C** warned **Treble Clef** about her and **Treble Clef** kept an eye on me the whole time."

"Yeah, I wouldn't want to cross **Treble Clef**. That **high pitch** of hers could be deadly."

"Enough about those two. Tell me all about your meeting with Lucious Caparoni."

"He is one of the coolest people I have ever met in my life, and I would like to be like him. His **voice** makes mine **sound** like mincemeat, Debra! I envy him in that he didn't care if anyone teased him about having a **high voice**. He loves to **sing**, and he doesn't care what people think. I think that's the one trait of his I'm really going to emulate."

"Did he tell you anything about his personal life, and did you get to sightsee?" Debra asked curiously.

"As you know, our time was very limited. However, I did manage to learn some interesting things about him. He was born on October 12 in Modena, Italy, and was an Italian **operatic tenor** who also crossed over into **popular music** and is probably one of the most successful **tenors** of all time."

"He was until you came along, Ted!" Debra said, winking at him.

"I don't know about that. It would take a miracle to accomplish all the things he has done."

"Tell me about Italy."

54

"I really only saw Modena, and not much of it. Lucious told me that if Italy were a meal, Modena would be the main course. It is a region of traditions having a passion for good cooking, and motors, and car design. Did you know it's famous for its balsamic vinegar, Debra?"

"No, I didn't know that! How did you do with the language?"

"Ohhh...thanks for asking! Did you get a **pitch pipe**, Debra?"

Debra couldn't help giggling and nodded her head with excitement!

"That was a big highlight of my trip, being able to communicate in a different language and understand them at the same time! Do you know how lucky we are to have those **pitch pipes**?"

"Yes, I do, Ted. When I was talking to my grandfather this morning, I asked him if he had received a **pitch pipe**, and he has one too. It is one miraculous tool!"

"Sorry to interrupt the two of you. However, we have arrived at the **conservatory**," **Middle C** announced.

Ted reached for Debra's hand and hurried to follow **Middle C** out of the **music** mobile. It was exciting to see their fellow students and hear the details of their trips. The only student who didn't seem to share their enthusiasm was Rita, and Debra couldn't help wondering if her know-it-all attitude finally got her into trouble. She tried not to inwardly gloat with thoughts of "serves her right," and "you get back what you dish out" but had a difficult time not feeling satisfaction that Rita had finally gotten a little taste of her own medicine. Her thoughts were interrupted when Mr. Walker excused them to go to their personal classes and Ted squeezed her hand when she turned to go into Brenda's classroom.

"Welcome back, Debra. It's great to see you!" Brenda replied happily when she saw Debra enter the room. "You look wonderful. How did everything go?"

"It was one of the best experiences I have ever had," and she proceeded to tell her all of the details of her trip!

"Wow, Debra. You should feel so honored! I have to tell you that **Treble Clef** was so excited about your trip, she shared your success story in one of our **staff** meetings! It is rare to receive high praise

CHRISTY WILBURN NOBELLA WEBB

like you got from Clyde Debosney, and I couldn't be more proud of you!"

"Thank you, Brenda. I wanted to also share with you that before I played 'Clarese le Dune' for him, I did the warm-up exercises you taught me, and he was extremely impressed with them! I gave you all the credit, and he told me to let you know he wished all teachers taught like you!"

"Well, thank you for sharing that, Debra. I have to say, that definitely made my day!"

"Here are the names of a couple of **pieces** he **played** for me, and, if it's okay with you, I would love to **learn** them."

"We can certainly find room for them in your **itinerary**."

Rita was having a miserable day and chalked it up to seeing Debra so happy with Ted's arm around her. Well, if all went according to her plan with Mildred, Debra would soon be **singing** an entirely different **tune**, and it couldn't come fast enough to suit her. It didn't help that her instructor corrected her for having a negative attitude and continued to reprimand her for not showing respect while on her recent trip. Rita wasn't used to being criticized and was not about to admit or apologize for any of her rude behavior. She thought for a moment. Had she been rude and disrespectful? Of course she had, but no one had the right to tell her she could improve her **flute play-ing**, especially when her parents had paid top dollar for her to **learn** from the best. It certainly wasn't her fault if her **performance** hadn't been flawless. She was just having an off day, and if it was anyone's fault, it was Debra's, not hers!

"How would you two like to spend an hour together while I run my errands?" **Middle C** asked before delivering them back home.

"We'd love that!" Ted and Debra spoke in **unison**.

"I figured you would enjoy some more time together. Let's **syn-chronize** our watches, and I'll be back in one hour **sharp**."

After seeing **Middle C** off, they turned to each other and slowly came together for a loving embrace followed by a passionate kiss. "I've definitely missed those lips of yours," Ted spoke lovingly.

"I was beginning to wonder if we were ever going to see each other again," Debra managed to say before meeting Ted's lips in another delightful kiss.

"I've missed you, Debra."

"And I've missed you, Ted. I can't believe next week is the beginning of another school year, and I'm not even excited about going! All I can think about is how much I'm going to miss seeing you."

"Thank heavens we have the weekends to look forward to, and I'm glad you have an understanding grandfather who will help us get that time we need to be together." He reached to pull her into his arms again, and they swayed back and forth while they clung to each other, each lost in their own thoughts.

"What is your schedule going to be like, Ted?"

"School starts next week for the junior high I work at, so I'll be back to a busier cleaning schedule, plus the regular hours I work at the Olive Garden. I don't start back to college for another two weeks. I do like being busy so I don't get down about missing you, Debra. It won't be like this forever, you know. We both have to concentrate on our schooling and do the things we need to do so we can have a good life together, right?"

"I know you're right, Ted, but it still doesn't make it any easier."

"I know it doesn't, sweetie."

"Oh, I like when you call me that, Ted," Debra said, looking into his deep brown eyes. They moved instinctively to each other's lips, sealing the space with their loving kiss and embrace. Debra hoped this moment would never end; however, like all good things, it eventually ended. "I'm so glad we had this chance to talk and hold each other."

They looked up in time to see **musical notes descending** around them, revealing **Middle C**'s imminent arrival. "I hope you two have had a pleasant hour, and now we need to depart," **Middle C** replied apologetically.

"We enjoyed our time and appreciate your allowing us to have it. Thanks, **Middle C**," Ted answered.

The flight back to Ted's **rest** stop was quiet while they held hands, once again lost in their individual thoughts. Before leaving,

Ted said, "Good luck at school, and I'll call you one night next week to see how everything's going, okay? You'll be on my mind constantly, sweetie. Don't forget that!" He leaned forward and gave her lips a kiss that promised many more good times to come.

Debra watched him leave and brushed at the tears that began to roll down her cheeks. Living in two different states was suddenly very hard, and she wasn't sure she would be able to survive this challenge.

When they arrived at her grandfather's house, **Middle C** could sense the change in her demeanor. "I'm sorry you're feeling down, Debra. Is there anything I can do?"

"You are so kind, Mr. **Middle C**. I wish there was something you could do; however, I'm afraid it's a problem that can only be worked out with time. I wish that Ted and I didn't live in two different states so it would be easier to see each other. We're lucky to have your magic to bring us together as often as we do. I'll be all right. I was just feeling sorry for myself for a minute. I think I'll get started on another new **piece** by Debosney, and it should do wonders for my blues!"

"That's my girl! You take care, Debra, and I'll see you again soon."

She watched until the last **note** disappeared back inside the old **player piano** and decided she better check her appearance since she had been crying. Wiping away the mascara tracks, she took a deep breath, and then turned out the lights to the **music** room, slowly climbing the stairs back to the kitchen. She nearly fainted with surprise when she opened the door and saw Mildred seated at the kitchen table with her grandfather.

"Hello, Debra! Long time no see," Mildred said with a slight sarcasm to her **voice**.

Temporarily speechless, she looked to her grandfather for help.

"Mildred stopped by with a little peace offering of cornbread, which I know you love, and we've been talking for a while. Why don't you pull up a chair and join us, Debra?"

"Oh, I wouldn't want to interfere, and my mother's expecting me back shortly," Debra managed to stammer, while thinking to herself that the last person she wanted to spend time with was Mildred!

"Well, at least let me cut you a slice that you can eat on your drive home," Mildred stated while slicing off a chunk of the cornbread.

It was difficult, but Debra somehow managed to courteously thank her and then followed her grandfather to the front door.

"Grandpa...I don't trust her," Debra whispered.

"I know, my dear. I'll be careful. Try not to worry." He kissed her gently on the forehead and watched her until she was in her car and safely pulling out of his driveway.

In the meantime, Mildred was in the kitchen gloating over the fact that the stage had been set and the plan she and Rita had devised was rolling out with phase one well underway!

Chapter 6

"Paul, I enjoyed spending time with you this evening. I've missed you so and hope we can get over our little misunderstanding. It was wonderful seeing Debra tonight, and even she seemed to be pleased about my being here to keep you company. I hope you'll read the vacation brochures I brought over for you and seriously consider going on this little road trip with me and the other seniors in our church group. We need to take advantage of every opportunity we can, especially at our age as we never know how much time we have left to do these things. Well, I don't want to wear out my welcome, so I'll be on my way now. If you'd like, I can stop by on my walk tomorrow, and we can get back in to exercising together. What do you think?"

"It all **sounds** good, Mildred, and I appreciate your stopping by. I would like to read up on that road trip before making a commitment. I'll need a few days to think about it. As far as the walking is concerned, I wouldn't mind getting back into the daily walks, so I'll look forward to walking with you tomorrow morning. Thanks again for the cornbread. It was delicious." He held the front door open for her and then walked her out to her car where he stood until she left.

While climbing the stairs to go back inside, he couldn't help remembering Debra's warning not to trust Mildred. He almost wished he hadn't opened the door to her when she knocked because he was finally adjusting to life without her in it. Would the drama begin all over again, or was he overreacting? He had to admit, he loved to travel, and from what he could see on the front of the brochures, it did look inviting!

Mildred couldn't believe how smoothly phase one of her plan with Rita was going! Paul was like putty in her hands, and she felt fairly positive she could convince him to go on the road trip. Once he made a commitment to go, she could then notify Rita, and phase two could be put into action!

Debra was having a terrifying nightmare, and the ringing of an alarm wouldn't stop. Someone was chasing her, and she was desperately trying to run; however, even though her feet were moving, she continued to stay in one place while the villain crept closer and closer. Just as he was about to grab her, she woke up realizing her nightmare was just a bad dream, and it was her alarm clock that was ringing, reminding her it was the first day of school! Breathing deeply, she was relieved it was only a dream and sat up to get her bearings, hoping the **rest** of her day would go better than the way it had started! Staring straight ahead in her room, she was grateful she had decided what she would wear the night before, and she gradually got moving, trying to get through the **movements** to get ready for the day ahead.

When Debra walked into the kitchen for breakfast, she still felt like her head was in a fog. "Good morning, Debra, is everything okay?" her mother asked, looking at her with a concerned look.

"I woke up having the worst nightmare today! I sure hope that's not an indication of how my day is going to go!"

"I'm sure it's just a sign of the first-day-of-school jitters, honey. Eat some breakfast and you'll get feeling better in no time at all."

"I'll take your word on that," Debra answered and sat down to eat her breakfast. Things seemed to go better after that, and soon she was waving goodbye to her family and running out the door to catch the school bus.

Mildred was rounding the corner to Paul's neighborhood and hoped she hadn't applied too much perfume that morning. She loved the flowery scent; however, she had been told by some of her senior friends that she should go easy on the amount she put on every day. Oh, what did they know—busybodies! When she looked up, she saw Paul walking out of his door, ready to join her.

Putting on one of her best smiles, she said, "Good morning, Paul, how are you doing today?"

"So far, so good. How are you, Mildred?"

"I couldn't be better! Fit as a **fiddle**!"

They were off to a good start, and as much as Mildred wanted to question him about the road trip, she refrained from doing so, lest she upset him, causing him to give her a definite no for an answer.

Debra couldn't believe it was lunchtime already and was relieved her day was going much better than she had anticipated. She closed her locker after swapping out the books she would need for her afternoon classes and walked quickly down the hall to meet Patty by the lunchroom door. "I'm so disappointed we don't have any classes together this year, Debra. How did your morning go?"

"So far it has gone well. I started my day off with a scary nightmare, so I've been worried since I got up this morning that my first day of school was going to be a disaster.

"And?"

"And I'm happy to report that it's been a pretty good day. Of course, it would've been better if we could've had some classes together!"

"I'll munch to that. Speaking of munching, thank goodness we both have the first lunch hour together! Mike has the second lunch hour, and I'm thinking it's probably because he's a year ahead of us in school." Patty moaned. "He informed me that his first football game is next Friday night! Please say you'll be going with me so we can cheer him and his friends on at the game! If we're really lucky, we can probably talk them into taking us out for something to eat after the game!"

In years past, Debra would have been as enthusiastic as Patty, but since meeting Ted, she didn't want to encourage the attention of any other guys.

"You don't act very excited, Debra," Patty pouted while waiting for her to answer.

"It's not that, Patty. It's just that I have feelings for Ted, and I'm not sure how he would feel if I was out dating other guys. I know I wouldn't be very happy if he was out with another girl."

"I totally forgot about Ted. He could come to the game too. Why don't you invite him?"

Moaning inwardly, Debra wondered how to explain the situation between Ted and herself. "Well, it's a little complicated."

"How complicated can it be? Most guys I know love football," Patty said impatiently.

"Well, he doesn't exactly live in Utah. He lives in California. He just happened to be visiting when I met him," Debra explained, thinking that was about the best way she was going to be able to explain their situation.

"Oh, that does complicate matters. Now, Debra, don't get mad or take this the wrong way, but maybe you should try to meet some new guys…and get a boyfriend who lives here. I can't imagine how awful that would be trying to have a long-distance relationship. I'm sure Mike has a lot of cool friends he could introduce you to. Just say the word, and I'll have him line you up."

"Thanks, but no thanks. I'd rather keep Ted and work things out my way."

"Well this certainly isn't how I pictured things would be going this year, Debra. In fact, it's going to be a little awkward. I'd really stop and think through this whole predicament you've got yourself in if I were you…and maybe reconsider your options!"

Debra wanted to scream at Patty, but tried to keep her cool. "I'll definitely give it some thought, Patty, and for sure I want to go to the game. Ted told me he'd call me later this week, so I can talk to him about the situation and then go from there."

The atmosphere between them seemed a little strained, but Debra had a right to like the guy she wanted to. Deciding to change the subject so things could cool down between them, Debra began talking about clothes and the latest fads, and soon the problem of Ted living so far away faded into the background.

The middle of the week found Debra busy doing homework when her mother called her to the telephone. With her heart **beating** faster, she hoped it was Ted. "Hello."

"How's my sweetie?"

"Oh, Ted, it's so good to hear your **voice**! I'm doing good. How's my guy?"

"I'm doing great and missing you like crazy! How's your first week of school going?"

"It's going okay, lots of homework already. I can't wait for Saturday to come so I can go over to my grandfather's and hopefully summon **Middle C** so we can spend a little time together. How has your week been going?"

"I've been busy too with the first week of school. The junior high has me constantly cleaning and moving desks and chairs around. Yesterday I went and **registered** for the fall semester at Orange Coast College. I'm looking forward to Saturday too. Hopefully you can summon **Middle C** early in case the Olive Garden schedules me for an early afternoon shift."

"I'm glad you let me know. I'm sure I can talk my grandfather into letting me summon **Middle C** first so we have a chance to see each other, and I can always clean his home when I get back. Speaking of which, you're never going to believe what has happened!"

"What happened?" Ted asked concerned.

"After **Middle C** dropped me off, I went upstairs and sitting at the kitchen table with my grandfather was Mildred, of all people!"

"No way!"

"I still can't believe it either. She made him a peace offering of cornbread and was telling him they just had a slight misunderstanding, no big deal. My grandfather invited me to sit down with them and have some cornbread, but I wasn't having any part of that, telling him I needed to get home. On my way out the front door, I warned him not to trust her. I don't know if it did any good or not. I just know she's up to something, and whatever it is, it's not going to be good!"

"I'm afraid I have to agree with you there. Well, now that we're back from our **music** trips, we need to meet with **Middle C** and get serious about figuring out what we're going to do before things get out of hand. I think we need to schedule some time to talk to **Middle C** this Saturday, even if it means we have less private time."

"I hate doing that, but under these **arrangements**, it doesn't leave us any other choice. Be thinking about what we can do so we can keep our meeting short."

"I will do that, sweetie. Don't forget you're always on my mind. I hate to have to run, but I am working in an hour and have to get ready. You be safe and before we know it, Saturday will be here."

"Thanks so much for calling, Ted. You mean the world to me. See you soon! Bye for now."

It was difficult to get back in the mood for studying, especially when she just wanted to think about Ted, with his big brown eyes and dazzling smile! Hurry, Saturday, you need to get here fast!

When Saturday morning arrived, Debra was tired and very tempted to sleep in because of getting up early for school every day; however, when she remembered that Ted might have to go to work earlier than usual, that was enough to jump-start her out of bed. She was relieved that her mother didn't question her and accepted her explanation that she needed to go and clean her grandfather's home early so she could also pick up Mrs. Martin's ironing in the afternoon.

"Good morning, Debra!"

"Good morning, Grandpa! I came over a little earlier hoping to talk to you for a few minutes."

"I bet I can guess what you want to talk to me about first."

"If you're hinting around about Mildred, you're absolutely right! What gives, Grandpa?"

"All I can tell you is I heard someone knock on my door, I opened it, and there stood Mildred, plain and simple. She looked so sad and miserable that I took pity on her, inviting her in. Of course, you know I have a weakness for cornbread, like a certain granddaughter of mine. What was I supposed to do?"

"You should have slammed the door in her face! What if she had poisoned you?"

"Now, now, Debra, aren't you going a little too far with your accusations?"

"I wish I could believe she was being sincere and had your best interest at heart, but there's just something that's not quite right about that woman."

Paul remembered the brochures Mildred had left, along with her invitation to go on a road trip, and was thankful he had placed them in a drawer. The last thing he needed now was for Debra to see them, causing another interrogation, especially if she knew he had made up his mind to go!

"Grandpa, would it be okay with you if I summon **Middle C** before cleaning your home? Ted called me during the week and told me there was a chance he could be called in on an early shift at the Olive Garden, and we were really hoping to spend a little time together. I promise I will work hard and get everything done that you need me to do when I get back."

"Of course, Debra, I trust you. You may want to start a load of wash and sort some clothes downstairs before summoning **Middle C**. Mildred and I have started walking again, and if by some small chance she went downstairs, we can justify your being down there to do the wash."

"And that's another thing, Grandpa, why do you have to justify anything to her? This is your house, and you or I shouldn't have to justify anything to Mildred! Oh, I'm afraid we're going right back to the way things were, and I'm very worried! Please promise me you'll be careful! I couldn't bear it if anything happened to you, Grandpa!"

"Nothing's going to happen to me, dear girl. Now I suggest you run along and get started before you lose any more precious time."

Debra walked over and gave her grandfather a tender kiss on the cheek while hugging him gently and then quickly left the room to gather up several bundles of wash.

"Hello, Debra! This is an early meeting time for you. Have you got a busy day ahead?"

"Yes, Mr. **Middle C**. I talked to Ted in the middle of the week, and he thought it would be a good idea to meet early in case he has to work an early shift. I hope you can take me to his **rest** stop."

"It would be my pleasure to be of service. Shall we go?"

"Yes, and the sooner, the better. The last time you dropped me off, Mildred was waiting to shock me when I went upstairs. Can you believe that? She and my grandfather have started walking again, and she could make an appearance anytime now."

"Oh dear, dear, dear. I was really hoping we had seen the last of her. Pardon my manners for saying so, Debra, but she is very unpredictable."

"I totally agree with you and have even begged my grandfather not to trust her, but it seems he thinks she deserves another chance. Mr. **Middle C**, I believe she is up to something, and so does Ted. We think we need to meet together **pronto** and are hoping you can join Ted and I to decide what **movement** or **theme** we need to **compose** to combat whatever **arrangements** she may be planning."

"I'm glad you decided to meet early because I do have an opening in my busy schedule, which will allow us to settle this **score** once and for all and **mute** any future **measures** she may devise." Pulling his **metronome** from his inside jacket pocket, he quickly turned the knobs, and seconds later, they were in the **music** mobile flying to Ted's **rest** stop.

Ted, Debra, and **Middle C** wrapped up their **impromptu** meeting and were each in **unison** for what needed to be done and what part they would be **playing**. "I think our theme is first-rate and should provide the **minor interlude** we need until further developments occur by Mildred and her **ensemble**, if she has any. Of course, my hope is that our **prelude** planning is for emergency **backup** and only used if absolutely necessary. It is my natural desire that this whole upsurge with Mildred falls **flat** on its face, and either she goes on her merry way, or she stops repeating her detestable behavior. Now then shall we move forward to a more cheerful topic? I'm sure you two would like a little alone time, and I do have a quick errand

CHRISTY WILBURN NOBELLA WEBB

that I need to run. Shall we **synchronize** our timepieces, and I will return in approximately a half hour?"

"Thank you, **Middle C**, for everything," Ted said, after checking his watch. "I totally agree with the **arrangements** we have come up with and will be on the lookout for anything that seems amiss. Debra and I appreciate some time to talk so we can catch up on each other's lives, and we'll keep our eye on the time so we don't cause you any delays."

After waving goodbye to **Middle C**, they quickly retreated to each other's arms, both eager to give and receive a hug and kiss. When a few moments had passed, Debra said, "I sure wish we didn't have to worry about Mildred. It was so nice to have her out of our lives for a few weeks."

"Shhhh, Debra, let's use our precious time to talk about us. I think we've done enough talking about Mildred for one day. I just want to hold you and look into your beautiful face."

Debra couldn't help but smile and welcomed his lips to hers for another kiss. The sun was shining, and so was her heart as they enjoyed the valuable time they had left in each other's company.

"Oh, Paul, I'm so elated about your decision to go on the road trip! I know you won't regret it! Several people mentioned they have gone on this trip before and have nothing but good things to say about it. My only regret is we have to wait several more weeks before we can go. I'm ready right now, aren't you?" Mildred barely heard Paul's response, too busy with thoughts of calling Rita to tell her the good news so they could begin the next phase of their plan!

Chapter 7

"Congratulations, Mildred! I have to admit I am a little surprised by your quick **movement** in implementing phase one based on what you told me about your relationship with Debra's grandfather. It was my understanding that you had a very difficult task ahead of you with your recent fallout with him. Be that as it may, I am thrilled that we can now put phase two into action. You do remember what I need you to do, don't you?"

"Yes, Rita, I wasn't born yesterday," Mildred snapped.

"Now, Mildred, don't use that **staccatoey tone** with me," Rita countered with a threatening growl in her **voice**.

Mildred immediately backed down, knowing there was one place she never wanted to find herself, and that was on Rita's bad side. She almost felt sorry for Debra, almost.

Debra was settling into a comfortable routine with school and was pleased that she was keeping up with her daily homework assignments. It was a challenge, but she was also trying to fit in time to **practice** so she would be able to continue her **studies** at the **conservatory**. The football game was tomorrow night, and she hadn't made up her mind yet on what to do about going with Patty and her friends to eat after the game. She couldn't help thinking about last year and how much easier it had been before Patty and Mike became an item. Back then, they all went out to eat as friends, and no one paired up together where things became serious. She thought back to the conversation she had had with Ted about always being honest and knew she needed to talk to him about this subject. As if on **cue**, the phone rang, and her mother told her it was for her.

"Hi, Debra, this is Ted. How's your week going?"

"Hi, Ted! I've had a pretty good week. How are things going for you?"

"It's been a good week for me as well and busy. I had an opportunity to pick up a couple of extra shifts at the Olive Garden, which helps make the time go by faster."

Debra **paused** uncomfortably, wondering how to bring up the subject of going to the football game.

"You're not very talkative tonight, Debra. Is everything okay?"

"Yes, everything's fine, Ted. Remember how we promised we would always be honest with each other?"

"Yes, I remember," Ted said with some concern in his **voice**.

"Tomorrow night is my school's first football game, and my best friend Patty's boyfriend is on the football team. I've been invited to go to the game and out to eat with a large group of friends."

"Did you think that I would be mad about that?"

"I wasn't sure how you would feel about it to tell you the truth. Before I met you, I would have loved to have gone, but now I feel like I'm betraying your trust."

"Why do you think you're betraying my trust, Debra?"

"I'm sorry, Ted, I guess I'm new at all this dating stuff."

"I knew this situation would come up eventually. Let's face it, you're a very attractive girl with a lot to offer. We both still need to date a lot before we settle down with that one and only person."

Debra thought her heart would break when she pictured Ted dating someone else and wasn't sure if her legs were going to support her. "So what are you saying, Ted?"

"What I'm saying is it's not fair for me to expect you not to date. You are at the age where you should be having fun and dating lots of guys, and I don't have the right to tie you down. It's hard for me to say that, but I think you need to go, and I want you to have fun and don't worry about how I'm going to feel about it."

Debra couldn't believe what she was hearing and wondered if Ted really had any feelings for her! "Are you going to start dating too, Ted?"

"Well, that's different, I don't think I need to date."

Debra was immediately relieved; however, the more she thought about it, the more it didn't seem fair for her to be dating and him to be staying home. This dating business was getting more complicated by the minute! "Ted, this is really hard. I have to admit I don't want either of us to date, but I know we're both still too young to be exclusive. I'm just not sure what the right answer is."

"Why don't we just leave it open for each of us to decide what is best. Speaking for myself, I'm not out there looking for anyone, but in your case, if someone asks you out, I think you need to go. I don't want a situation where someday either one of us regrets the fact that we didn't take the opportunity to date when we could have and then be sorry that we didn't. Do you understand what I'm trying to say, Debra?"

"Yes, I understand, and I also hate hearing what you're saying. I already told Patty I'm not interested in dating anyone, but wouldn't mind going out with a group of friends. My heart belongs to you, Ted."

"I'm glad to hear that, Debra, and I can honestly say that my heart belongs to you too. I don't want you to miss out on your high school activities. They're very important."

"I'm lucky that you are so understanding Ted. I just hope you don't feel like you need to go out with Rita! I don't think I could take that."

"That makes two us! I don't think you have anything to worry about there. Are you getting in any **practice** time, Debra?"

"Yes, I'm managing to squeeze in a few minutes here and there when I need a break from my homework. My **music** does a lot to help me relax. Are you still **singing**?"

"I **sing** all the time, and I'm loving it. I know people probably stare at me and think I've lost it, but I don't let it bother me anymore."

"I'm sure they're loving your **singing**! They're probably staring because they can't believe someone can **sing** as incredible as you do!"

CHRISTY WILBURN NOBELLA WEBB

"That's my girl, always making me feel on top of the world! Well, sweetie, I hate to say it, but I better be going for now. I'm looking forward to Saturday and spending time with you. I'll talk to you later."

"Goodbye, Ted, and thanks for being you!"

After ending her phone call, she had mixed emotions. Ted was always supportive and understanding of whatever she was going through, which she loved of course. The bad part was she couldn't stand the thought of him going out with anyone else but her and admitted that was pretty selfish on her part.

Debra woke up during the night with a bad dream of seeing Ted on a date with Rita. When she saw them moving closer together for a kiss, she'd seen enough and sat up in bed. This dating stuff was a lot harder than she had ever imagined, and she wondered again for the umpteenth time if she would survive it.

As she went about her day, the dream she'd had about Ted and Rita constantly seemed to haunt her thoughts, and she looked forward to the football game, hoping to focus her mind on something else. Patty was thrilled when she heard she was going to the game and even happier when she agreed to get something to eat afterward with their group of friends. Seeing her enthusiasm, seemed to be exactly what Debra needed to help pull her out of her gloomy mood.

The game was a nail-biter, with each team staying neck and neck until the last few seconds of the game when Skyline's Mike kicked for a field goal, made it, and pushed them ahead with a final **score** of 24 to 21. Debra rode with Patty over to Hardy's for the victory celebration, and Patty was on cloud nine over Mike being the hero and saving the day with the winning goal.

By the end of the evening, Debra had to admit she was glad she went. It was fun to get out and mingle with friends she hadn't seen since school let out last spring, and she even met some new friends. She managed to avoid most of the guys all night, that was until Matt came up and pushed his way into a spot next to her. He had an unforgettable **low bass voice**, and she couldn't help thinking about their conversation. "Where have you been hiding all night?"

Debra was shocked when he asked the question and turned around to see who he was talking to. "You don't need to turn around. I'm talking to you, Strawberry red!"

She couldn't help giggling when he called her "Strawberry red," knowing he was referring to her hair color, and he had a slight accent when he spoke. "I haven't been hiding all night. You just haven't been looking my way until now."

"Well, if I'd known you was sooo perty, I would have made my way here a lot sooner. I happen to be very attracted to redheads!"

"Is that so?"

"Yes it is so. May I have the pleasure of knowing your name, or should I just call you 'Strawberry'?"

"My name is Debra, but you can call me Strawberry if you want to. And you are?"

"My name is Matthew, but my friends call me Matt. I'm new to the area, moved here from Dallas, Texas. You may have noticed a slight accent when I speak. I'm working on it, but it seems to follow me around."

"Well, don't change it. I think it's nice, and it suits you, Matt." Her eyes **studied** him, realizing he was a little taller than Ted, with light blond hair and the palest blue eyes she'd ever seen. He had a warm smile with straight white teeth, and he was well-built, with broad shoulders and narrow hips. "Welcome to Utah, Matt. Do you like it here?"

"I'm liking it more and more now that I've met you," he said with a wink.

"I bet you say that to all the girls you meet," Debra interrupted him with a laugh.

"Not all the girls. They're not as perty as you!"

Debra rolled her eyes, and he continued with, "I love the mountains and plan to go snow skiing in the winter. Do you ski, Debra?"

"No, I don't like to be cold. All my friends think I'm crazy, especially since we have the best snow on earth, but I'd just rather spend my hard-earned money on other things."

"Yeah, like what other things?"

Debra was about to answer when Patty told her she was ready to drive her home and needed to leave now because Mike was going to meet her at her home after dropping her off.

"It was nice talking to you, Matt. I need to go now. My ride home is leaving."

"It was nice meeting you, Strawberry, and I hope to see more of you in the future."

She saw Patty raise her eyebrows and then give her a wink. Debra waved at Matt and hurried to follow Patty out. "Okay, girl, fill me in on what that was all about!" Patty said eagerly. "I knew you'd find a new guy here."

"Now, Patty, don't go jumping to any conclusions. I only talked to him for a few minutes. My heart still belongs to Ted!"

"Well, from where I'm sitting, that may be short lived."

"Trust me, Patty, I don't move as fast as you do! And for your information, I did talk to Ted about going out after the football game, and he encouraged me to do so and date if I want to."

"If Mike said that to me, I would be very suspicious and would probably hire a detective to see who he's dating!"

"Ted and I aren't dating exclusively yet. We both realize we're still too young to not date others, so if an occasion comes up, we've agreed that we should date others in order to make sure we're still right for each other."

"Well, that's the dumbest thing I've heard yet. I can guarantee you now that I'll never have that kind of an agreement with Mike. The day he suggests something that ridiculous is the day I give him his walking papers!"

Debra was relieved when they finally pulled up in front of her house. "Thanks for the ride, Patty. You and Mike have a good time. I'll see you later."

Debra lay in bed for what seemed like hours and wondered if sleep would ever come because her mind wanted to keep re**playing** the conversations she had had that night. The one conversation that stood out the most was the one she had had with Matt. Just thinking about it, made her heart start **beating** with excitement, and it confused her because she thought she was in love with Ted. While trying to picture Ted in her mind, the last thing she remembered before drifting off to sleep were pale blue eyes!

Chapter 8

Debra got up early Saturday morning, partly because she couldn't sleep very well, and she was anxious to get her day started so she could get over to her grandfather's house. While getting dressed, she struggled to keep thoughts of Matt out of her mind and instead tried to concentrate on seeing Ted, wondering what would be in store for them at the **conservatory** today.

Her mother hardly noticed what time it was when she announced she was leaving, handing her a bowl of potato salad sealed in a Tupperware dish to give to her grandfather. The drive over was relaxing, and she arrived feeling excited about her day.

"Good morning Debra!" her grandfather greeted her cheerfully. "Are you cleaning first or going to the **conservatory** first?"

"Going to the **conservatory** first. However, I'll get the clothes sorted and the wash started before I leave. Good thinking?"

"Excellent thinking, my dear!" Her grandfather smiled, winking at her.

"Before I forget, I have a care package from my mother for you." She handed him the Tupperware dish.

"Wow, it looks like your mother's famous potato salad! I don't know if I can wait for lunch. I may have to sample some now!"

"It's all yours, Grandpa. Help yourself!" She was on a tight time schedule, and as much as she wanted to question her grandfather about the latest news on Mildred, time didn't permit it.

Soon the wash was started, and she summoned **Middle C.**

"Good morning, Debra. I hope you're having a good Saturday. Do you have any news to report regarding Mildred?"

"Nothing new that I'm aware of, Mr. **Middle C**. I didn't have time to question my grandfather about her this morning, but I'll try to get an update before I go back home today."

"Splendid! Shall we be off?"

"**Sounds** good to me." It didn't take long to become airborne, and Debra concentrated on calming her nerves, not wanting to alert Ted that anything had changed about her.

When Ted boarded the **music** mobile, he held roses in his hand and smiled warmly at her as he came down the aisle. "Beautiful flowers for my beautiful lady! How are you, Debra?"

All the emotions that had been worrying her up to that point instantly vanished in his kind gesture. "Thank you, Ted! You are so thoughtful, and you know I love these colors."

"They remind me of good memories we've made, and the peach especially reminds me of your beautiful hair! Sooo…how was the football game?"

"We won our first game! It was one of those games that keeps you on the edge of your seat. My friend Patty's boyfriend kicked the winning field goal, so she was on cloud nine all night!"

"Did you go out to eat with your friends?"

"I did, and I was glad I went. I saw a lot of people that I hadn't seen over the summer, and it was fun catching up on what everyone's been doing." She conveniently left out the part about meeting Matt. At this point, she didn't know if anything was going to come of it. She was relieved that she felt happy to be with Ted and was ready to focus all her attention on him.

They both felt the familiar jolt of their landing and stood ready to leave the **music** mobile. Debra held her roses in one hand and clutched Ted's hand in her other. When they walked into the meeting room of the **conservatory**, she immediately felt Rita's eyes shooting daggers her way. It surprised her when she didn't feel the familiar pains of jealousy she normally felt, especially when she noticed Rita dressed in the latest fashion, with not a hair out of place, but instead smiled with confidence as Ted led them to their seats. It felt good to know she could attract more than one guy; after all, Matt was handsome, and he even told her she was 'perty!'

She had an amazing day in class, and Brenda gave her helpful tips on how to work out her **fingering** on a difficult section of the new **piece** of **music** Clyde Debosney had suggested she might enjoy. The other half of the class time was spent on **theory** since the first week of school had preempted her **practice** time.

On their flight back to Ted's **rest** stop, **Middle C** mentioned that an unusual **development** had occurred while they were attending their classes. He explained that he had been approached by **Largo**, who was Rita's **mentor**, and was asked if Rita and Debra were on good terms. "As you can imagine, I immediately asked him why he would ask me such a question."

"Well, don't keep us in suspense, **Middle C**. What gives?" Ted prodded.

"He advised that Rita had made a special request of him right before your **music** tours to drop her off near Debra's grandfather's home, stating that she was meeting Debra so they could coordinate their plans for their upcoming tours."

"I never met Rita before we went on our **music** tours," Debra replied, looking puzzled.

"Oh wow, that's crazy," Ted answered. "What do you think she was up to, **Middle C**?"

"It's disturbing, but if I were to venture a guess, I would say, she is possibly in cahoots with our conniving Mildred."

"No way!" Ted and Debra responded in **unison**.

"Can you two think of a better reason for her wanting to be dropped off in that location?" **Middle C** asked.

"Well, no," Ted responded in deep thought. Debra was too shocked to even reply.

"I couldn't either and felt it imperative that I bring it to your attention **pronto** so we can be on the lookout for any **movement** on her part, and on Rita's as well. I'm sorry to be the bearer of bad news, but a **measure** of caution is worth a pound of cure, wouldn't you agree?"

"Yes, you're right, **Middle C**, and from now on we better not take anything for granted."

For the remainder of their flight to Ted's **rest** stop, you could have heard a pin drop with the **silence** that occurred while each contemplated what Rita could possibly be up to.

"I'm sorry, Debra. I know this news is upsetting. Are you going to be okay?" Ted asked with concern.

"I don't know. It seems like every time things start going good, something like this happens. I'm not sure how to react or what I should prepare for. Do you know what I mean?"

"Yes, I do. That's why I'm worried. I want you to promise me that you'll take time to be aware of your surroundings, and don't take anything for granted," Ted said, kissing her gently on her cheek as he stood to leave.

Debra followed him on his way out and took a seat closer to **Middle C**. "What do you think will happen, Mr. **Middle C**?"

"I wish I knew so I could prepare us all for whatever may come. For now, we'll just have to take things one **note** at a time."

"I wish it was that easy," Debra mumbled while stepping out of the **music** mobile. She waved goodbye to **Middle C**, and after putting the washed clothes into the dryer and placing a new batch into the washer, she gathered her things and went upstairs. She carefully opened the door into the kitchen and stood still, **listening** for any sign that her grandfather was in the house. Not hearing anything, she assumed he must be out on his daily walk with Mildred and decided the sooner she got busy with the cleaning, the better off she'd be if they were to come home. She was just finishing up the bathrooms when she heard the front door open and her grandfather's **voice** inviting Mildred to come in. She hoped Mildred would be too busy, but unfortunately, she heard Mildred tell him she would love to.

Putting on her best behavior, she greeted them with, "Hello, you two! How was your walk today?"

"It's a gorgeous morning, and we've just come back from an invigorating walk, wouldn't you agree, Mildred?"

"Yes indeed, Paul, most exhilarating!" Mildred turned toward Debra and in a slightly mocking **tone** asked, "And what have you been up to this morning, Debra?"

Forcing herself to keep her temper under control and remaining calm, Debra responded cheerfully, "I've been working on the wash, changed my grandfather's bed, and I just finished cleaning the bathrooms. Grandpa, did you want me to mop the kitchen floor today?"

"Why don't we leave that job for next week? I want to make sure you have enough time to vacuum, and instead of dusting, would you mind polishing the furniture? It really needs it."

"No problem, I'll do that next after I put the last load of wash into the dryer." With that, she skipped out of the room before Mildred could come up with anything else to accuse her of. All the way downstairs, Debra wanted to yell to the world how much she disliked Mildred, screaming to the top of her lungs that she wasn't fooling her for one second, and furthermore, she was aware that she was plotting and scheming to do her in with her no good partner, Rita!

Well, bring it on, you old battle-ax, 'cause I'm ready for you!

Mildred was smiling inwardly, thinking it wouldn't be long now before things would be going her way and the spoiled, bratty Debra would get what she finally deserved! She must have been smiling a little too much because Paul interrupted her thoughts by saying, "It sure is nice to see you happy and getting along with Debra!"

Mildred almost choked but caught herself in time, replying, "Well, thank you, Paul, for noticing. I was also thinking about our upcoming road trip and how much fun we're going to have. I can't help smiling every time I think about it."

Debra spent Saturday afternoon doing the Martins' ironing, and unfortunately there weren't any good movies on TV, so most of her time was spent thinking about the information **Middle C** had revealed earlier about Rita having **Largo** drop her off near her grandfather's house. What could those two be up to? The one thing she did discover was when you're an honest person, it's practically next to impossible to come up with something that's sneaky and under-handed when it totally goes against your nature to be that way. It was a relief when she heard the telephone ring, and she hoped it was Ted when her mother called her to the phone.

"Hello," she answered in her most pleasant **voice**.

"Hello, Strawberry, can you guess who this is?"

Debra's heart definitely skipped a **beat** when she heard the Texas accent, and she knew immediately it had to be Matt. "Well, hello, Matt, how are you on this Saturday afternoon?"

"Hey, Strawberry, you recognized my **voice**! I am doing fantastic and would be doing even better if you would agree to let me take you out on a date this evening. What would you say to that?"

"Tell me what you have in mind," Debra said while quickly glancing down at her appearance and hoping she would have enough time to put herself together.

"A group of friends thought it would be fun to get together and **play** some games at your friend Patty's house while eating chips and dip. I could pick you up around seven, and we'd probably be out till eleven or twelve. Would you like to go?"

"I think it **sounds** like a lot of fun. Could you hold on a moment while I check with my parents?"

"Of course I will, Strawberry."

Debra put the phone down and hurried to the kitchen to tell her mother what was happening. "I think that **sounds** fun, Debra, and you have my permission to go."

Debra hurried back to the phone.

"Matt, I have permission to go, and I'm looking forward to it."

"Well, Strawberry, you just made my day! I will see you at seven **sharp**."

She rushed back to finish her ironing, now lost in thoughts about the evening ahead. It felt good to forget about the troublesome Mildred and focus her thoughts on more interesting things. She had to admit there was something irresistible about Matt, and she looked forward to spending the evening with him.

Rita sighed with relief when she saw her friend Angie pull into the parking lot of the Olive Garden where Ted worked. She had called earlier in the day to see if Ted was scheduled to work and was pleased when she found out he would be working the dinner shift until closing. She needed Angie's help in moving into phase two where Ted was concerned.

"Hello, Rita, you're looking fabulous tonight," Angie said when she saw her friend.

"Did you expect anything less from me, Ang?"

"Of course not, but you do surprise me with the length you'll go to in order to make a good impression." Angie couldn't help admiring the maroon jumpsuit that hugged Rita's every perfect curve tightly, accentuating her tiny waist and shapely hips and legs. Her hair glowed, having been freshly weaved, and her blonde highlights were curled just right in order to hang flawlessly down her back and wave around her face. It was obvious that she had taken extra time on her makeup as her eye shadow was applied with flawlessness, and each eyelash was brushed with mascara to precision exactness. Her cheeks and lips glowed with picture-perfect color, and she looked like she had just stepped out of a glamour magazine. There was no denying her exquisite appearance when all eyes turned in her direction as they entered the restaurant and walked forward to be seated.

Rita didn't miss a **beat**, informing the hostess that she had called in earlier that day to be seated at one of Ted's tables. They quickly followed the hostess to Ted's section, and Angie couldn't help noticing all the attention Rita was attracting as they walked to their table. Ted was informed immediately that "royalty" had just been seated in his service area and he better be quick about getting them served. Not sure what all the hullabaloo was about, he hurried over to see who had just been seated at one of his tables.

"Great," Ted muttered to himself when he saw Rita and Angie. "Looks like I'm in for a long night tonight!" Doing his best to put on a positive, professional attitude, he walked up to greet his two new guests. "Well, good evening, ladies, it's always a pleasure to see you at the Olive Garden. What can I get you started on tonight?"

"You shouldn't ask questions you're not prepared to satisfy, Ted!" Rita replied with a suggestive look. Angie joined in with a wicked laugh, and Ted wanted to have nothing to do with either one of them; however, knew he still had to behave courteously in order to keep his job.

"Now, ladies, let's not go there. I'm referring only to what you'd like to start off drinking tonight." After **listening** to their woeful cries of protest, he was finally able to take their order and scurried away to place it. While waiting in line to pick up their drinks, a fellow waiter asked, "Hey, Ted, how come you always get the gorgeous ladies? I wish some of your luck would rub off on me!"

Ted wished his luck would rub off on the other waiter too but didn't dare **voice** his thoughts. "You'll get lucky next time," Ted replied, wishing he would.

Debra yawned and then climbed into bed while thinking about her date with Matt. Her sides still ached from all the laughing she had done, not to mention her cheeks hurt from smiling all night. They played Crazy Eights and charades, and Patty's mother outdid herself with chips and dip, as well as homemade ice cream and chocolate chip cookies. Another couple had joined them, Connie and her date, Anthony. They were incredibly fun, which made the evening even more enjoyable. She had to admit it felt good to just relax and have fun and not think about crazy problems. Forgetting Rita and Mildred was the best medicine she could have taken to ease her worries. Smiling, she thought about Matt calling her Strawberry all night, and with his Texas accent, it was growing on her. His beautiful blue eyes were hard to ignore, and if she wasn't careful, she could get lost in them! Her eyelids were beginning to grow heavy now, and she knew sleep was just around the corner.

Rita and Angie had thoroughly enjoyed their dinner at the Olive Garden, and it went without saying that Rita couldn't keep her eyes off Ted. Once they had reached the parking lot, Rita turned to Angie and said, "Okay, Ang, are you sure you understand what I need you to do?"

CHRISTY WILBURN NOBELLA WEBB

"Yes, Rita, you've told me a bazillion times. I don't think I've ever seen you this obsessed with a guy before. It's kind of disturbing. Are you sure he's worth all this?"

"Ang, you're really beginning to get on my nerves. I'm asking one small favor of you, and the way you're acting, you'd think I'd asked for your firstborn."

"Well, thank heavens I don't have any children because I wouldn't put it past you to ask! Okay, **listen**, we're both tired, and I know what you need me to do. I'll do it and then let you know how it goes, okay?"

"When are you going to do it, Ang?"

"I'll see how my schedule goes, but either Monday or Tuesday, most likely Tuesday, okay?"

"I guess that will have to do. Just know I'll be waiting by my phone until I hear from you."

Angie rolled her eyes, letting Rita know her demanding favors were getting old. At this point, she didn't care if it cost her her friendship with Rita. Rita was only out for herself, and Angie was getting tired of being used by her. "I'm exhausted and need to be going now. I'll talk to you later, Rita." Angie could hear Rita mumbling as she walked away and decided this one-sided friendship wasn't worth it anymore.

Chapter 9

Debra was having a good week in school and was surprised how quickly the week was going by. While working on her math assignment in her bedroom, she heard the telephone ring Tuesday afternoon and hoped it might be Ted when her mother called her to the phone. "Hello, this is Debra," she replied after answering.

"Did you say your name was Debra?" the female **voice** said on the other end.

"Yes, who's calling please?" Debra quickly asked.

"You don't know me, but I felt that it was in your best interest that I call you and tell you some things about a guy named Ted. Do you know a Ted Nobson?"

"Yes, I know, Ted. How do you know him?"

"I put an ad in the help wanted section of the paper, and he responded to my request. I needed help moving some furniture and needed someone strong who could help me. I must say he is very strong, and not only that, he's handsome, with an incredible **voice**. My daughter loves **music** too, and they hit it off instantly when she heard him **humming** while moving my furniture. I wasn't concerned about their initial attraction to each other until I heard Ted mention that he had a girlfriend and hoped she wouldn't find out about him meeting my daughter. I don't know how serious you two are, but if the situation were reversed, I would appreciate it if someone let me know. I have always believed that honesty is the best policy."

Debra felt shocked at what she was hearing and certainly at a loss for words.

CHRISTY WILBURN NOBELLA WEBB

"Are you still there?" the **voice** on the other end asked.

"Yes…I'm still here. You didn't tell me your name."

"I'm sorry, my name is Angela. My friends call me Angie, and here is my phone number if you need to get in touch with me. I hope I haven't ruined your day, but like I said, if the situation were reversed, I would want to know. I'm going to hang up now. Goodbye, Debra."

Debra didn't feel very well after hanging up the phone and began to get a sick feeling in the pit of her stomach. Her emotions ran from hurt, anger, and a myriad of similar emotions in between. Part of her was upset and confused, but did she really have the right to be mad? After all she had gone out with Matt and found him quite attractive and didn't plan to say anything to Ted about him. How would he feel if he knew how much she enjoyed Matt's attention? Hadn't she given him permission to date as well? Wow, this dating stuff was really getting complicated. One thing she had been right about was going back to school had definitely changed things between them!

Rita pounced on the phone when it rang, willing it to be Angie.

"Hello, Rita, I'm calling to let you know I have completed your favor…and it's the last time I'm going to do something like this for you."

"Well, it's about time you called, Ang, and you can stop with the drama queen act. If a friend can't ask for a favor once in a while— oh, never mind! Just give me the details on what happened. Did it devastate the country bumpkin?"

"All I can tell you is she suddenly clammed up and became very quiet. I had to ask her if she was still there."

Rita burst into glorious laughter, absolutely enjoying every juicy detail. "Serves her right for all the pain and suffering she has put me through. Well, Ang, I have to run now. I have plans to put into motion, and I'm sure you have your own life to live. Seeing as how you don't want to do me any more favors, do us both a favor and don't call back. Forget you ever knew me!" Rita slammed the phone receiver back into its cradle, hoping the abruptness hurt Angie's **ear**. "Who needs her?" Rita said in a nasty **tone** and laughed while relifting the receiver to dial Mildred's number.

86

"Hello," Mildred said sleepily into the receiver after answering the phone.

"Mildred, what is wrong with you, and why are you sleeping in the middle of the day? Don't you know we have phase two to put into action? Honestly, the people I have to work with to get things done!"

"Rita, I am a lot older than you and can't go a hundred miles an hour like I used to."

"Well, could you at least try to get your motor started? I have a lot to do and don't have time to wait for slow people! I want an update on what's happening on your end, and I need it **pronto**!"

After **listening** to Mildred's update, Rita was satisfied and hoped she was telling her the truth. If so, things were a little ahead of schedule, and maybe she could go and get some beauty sleep herself, not that she needed it, of course!

Mildred yawned and scratched her head, trying to think what she should do first. She didn't want Rita mad at her and decided the sooner she took care of her end of the plan, the better off she'd be. Pulling out the yellow pages, she began scrutinizing the ads on how to dispose of an unwanted **piano**. She **drummed** her fingernails on the kitchen table while she carefully read and debated which option would work the best. She stopped immediately on the ad for the Salvation Army, deciding they would be the quickest and most efficient way for her to get rid of Paul's old **player piano**. Picking up her phone, she gave them a call and questioned them until she felt satisfied that all parties involved could handle the **arrangements**. She even went so far as to set up the appointment time and date to pick up the bothersome **piano**, as well as provide Paul's address. The next step was to nonchalantly get a **key** to his home so she could meet the **piano** movers. She would have to figure that part of the plan out later due to the pounding in her head from the onset of a new migraine headache.

Saturday was fast approaching, and Debra was feeling mixed emotions about whether she even wanted to see Ted. The conversation she had had with Angela earlier in the week would not stop **play-**

ing in her head, and as time moved closer to Saturday, she became more confused. Thank goodness it was Friday and the football game after school was being **played** at their home field, and with any luck, she might get to see Matt at the game or possibly after when they all went to get something to eat at Hardy's.

The game had just wrapped up with another victory for Skyline. Debra had taken care to wear the school colors of gold and blue, loving the way her gold sweater highlighted her strawberry blonde hair. She wore it over the top of her navy blue skirt and completed her outfit with her black-and-white saddle shoes. She was disappointed she hadn't seen Matt; however, she certainly didn't want to volunteer that little fact to Patty, who kept insisting she needed to forget Ted and move on with Matt. She had to admit, especially after the phone call she received earlier in the week, that it may not be such a bad idea.

Her heart started **beating** faster when she and Patty walked into Hardy's and she heard a familiar **voice** call out to "Strawberry," waving them over to sit at their table. Patty didn't give her a chance to sit anywhere else, and they soon joined Matt and his friends at their table. The energy in the room was charged up from the victory of the football game, and it was next to impossible to hear what anyone was saying. She didn't mind because it felt great to absorb all the positive energy in the room while forgetting Ted's possible rejection.

Before she had time to say no, Matt had pulled her to the dance floor, and they began dancing the twist, which felt great, and before she knew it, the **music** was helping her to get rid of the worries she was having over Ted. By the time the **song** ended, she was feeling much more relaxed and was more than happy to move into Matt's arms for the slow **song** that followed.

"Strawberry, have I told you how beautiful you look tonight?"

"You might have, but it's been so noisy in here, I didn't hear you," Debra replied while looking into the bluest eyes she had ever seen.

"Well, you are the pertiest girl I have ever seen." And he pulled her a little tighter as they continued dancing.

Debra looked at him and smiled. "Thank you, Matt! You have the pertiest blue eyes I have ever seen!" Before she realized it, he leaned down and gave her nose a kiss, moved to her cheek, kissing it gently, and then slowly moved his lips to hers. It was a wonderful kiss, and she couldn't help returning his affection. The **rest** of the evening moved by in a blur, and the thing she remembered most was the contentment she felt in Matt's arms.

Mildred arrived home and flopped into the nearest chair. While catching her breath, she thought about what she'd been up to for the past few hours. All week she had agonized over how she was going to get Paul's house **key** and get a copy of it without him knowing it. After suffering never-ending migraines, she finally decided the best thing to do would be to go and visit several locksmiths in the area to find out if there was a way they could make a copy without her having the actual **key** with her. Smiling, she thought about the step-by-step instructions the locksmith had given her on how she could accomplish this impossible feat! Who would have thought modeling clay and a rolling pin could be her best friend? Laughing, she worried if she wasn't careful, she'd soon be losing her mind!

After leaving the locksmith, she drove straight to the hardware store and purchased the items needed to pull off the next step of her escapade. Finally she made a stop at the market and bought ingredients for a tasty barbeque dinner she planned to host at her home, and while Paul was cooking the steaks, she would be putting the finishing touches on phase two. Now that she was **rest**ed and knew what to do, she hurried to the phone to call Paul and invite him to a barbeque at her home tomorrow evening.

Patty had just dropped Debra off at home, and she hurried inside. The light was on over the desk, and a **note** had been left by her mother advising that Ted had called. It was a little after eleven, and her parents had already gone to bed. She checked to make sure the front door was locked and turned off the lights before going down to her room. She wondered if Ted was going to the **conservatory** tomorrow or if she was supposed to call him back. What if he wanted to break up with her and was calling to let her know? With several thoughts racing through her head, she got ready for bed and decided to deal with whatever would come tomorrow.

Not sleeping very well, Debra didn't have a problem getting up early Saturday morning. While eating breakfast with her mother, she tried to get a few more details about Ted's phone call; however, he hadn't left any specifics about what he wanted to talk to her about. All she could think about was "no news is good news," and she would just have to proceed with caution.

Her grandfather seemed to be in a great mood when she arrived, and she could only guess that that meant he was madly in love with Mildred again. She really had to figure out what Mildred was up to and expose her for the witch she was. For now she concentrated on getting downstairs to summon **Middle C**. "Good morning, Miss Debra, how are things going for you this fine day?"

"I'm doing okay."

"I'm happy to hear that. However, something tells me that you could be better?"

"As I've always said, Mr. **Middle C**, you have a knack for always being able to read me."

"Well, please don't keep me in suspense. Aren't you going to enlighten me on whatever your dilemma is?"

"I wish I could, Mr. **Middle C**, but I'm not sure of what it is myself. I'm going to have to **play** things by **ear** today and see what **notes** appear, if you know what I mean."

"You know, dear girl, in order to do that, you have to possess a special **talent**. Do you possess that **talent**, Debra?"

"Let's just say in this particular case, it's a little more complicated. Someone I've never met before told me some things about Ted, and now I have to see if he will confirm or deny what I've heard."

"Oh dear, what if Ted is an innocent victim and doesn't even know he's in the middle of something? Did you stop to consider that?"

"Well, no, I didn't. I was so wrapped up with what was said that I just took it for granted that it was the truth. I think it's a good thing we had this talk, Mr. **Middle C**."

"You know I'm always happy to help, and with Rita and Mildred out to sabotage you and Ted, you need to examine all possibilities. However, time is flying by, and we better be on our way for now."

It didn't take long for **Middle C** to set his **metronome** for their **course**, and within seconds they were on their way. Debra was grateful she had talked to **Middle C** so she wouldn't accuse Ted of something he didn't do. She had already been Rita's victim once. The only thing that confused her was the person who called was Angela, not Rita. Could Angela be involved in helping Rita plot against her?

Debra **studied** Ted carefully when he got on the **music** mobile and didn't see anything different about him. "How's my girl today?" he asked, smiling.

"I'm doing pretty good. How are you doing?"

"I had a crazy busy week. I registered for all my classes and picked up a few extra shifts at the Olive Garden, which reminds me, I had another visit from Rita and her friend, requesting that I be their server at the Olive Garden."

"Really?" Debra said with a perplexed look on her face. "Ted, by chance, would her friend's name be Angela?"

"Rita calls her Angie, which could be short for Angela. Why?"

Debra then proceeded to tell Ted about her Tuesday afternoon phone call with all the details of his supposed flirting with Angela's daughter.

"Oh, that ticks me off," Ted replied angrily. "I had a feeling they were up to something. I really thought we had made it clear to Rita that she can't break us apart. So much for thinking, right? Debra, I hope you believe me and know that not a word of that phone call is true."

"I have to be truthful…I did believe it until I talked to **Middle C** this morning. He told me it was probably Rita or Mildred trying to come between us."

Their conversation got interrupted with their landing at the **conservatory**, and Ted reached out a hand to help her up. "Well, thank goodness for **Middle C**. I'm glad he knows what kind of a guy I am."

"Please don't be mad at me, Ted. You don't know how convincing she was. It's not easy being in two different states, and I'm human and can only take so much sometimes."

"Hey, you two, don't let Rita win by driving a wedge between the two of you. It **sounds** like you're letting her succeed."

Ted grabbed her hand, and they walked to class **silently**, each lost in their own thoughts.

Rita's smile faded considerably when she looked up and saw Ted and Debra holding hands as they walked in. *How can that be?* she thought angrily to herself. *If Ang called her like she said she did, why in the world are they holding hands? Something's not right here, and I'm going to get to the bottom of this!*

The **rest** of Debra's day was uneventful, and she spent her time cleaning her grandfather's house and was now home working on the Martins' ironing. She hoped Matt wouldn't call wanting to go out tonight because she wouldn't be very good company. Her thoughts strayed to Ted, thinking he didn't say much after class at the **conservatory**, and she guessed he was still upset with her for believing Angela's lie about him. She wished he could be in her shoes for a change, then he would understand what she was going through. After eating dinner, she decided to escape from her problems for a while with a good book she had recently purchased and headed for her room where she wouldn't be disturbed.

Mildred felt like a chicken with its head cut off, trying to get everything ready for her barbeque with Paul. If she didn't have to get a copy of his house **key**, she wouldn't be such a nervous wreck! Why in the world did she ever get herself mixed up with Rita in the first place? Her thoughts were immediately interrupted with the ringing of the doorbell.

All right, Mildred, show time! Better pull yourself together and get this dastardly deed done once and for all!

She took a deep breath to calm her nerves and walked anxiously to the door. "Hello, Paul, how are you this evening?" she greeted. "Won't you come in? I have some refreshing lemonade for us chilling in the refrigerator. Let me take your **keys** and sweater, and I'll place them on this side table here by the door while you pour us each a tall cool glass of lemonade." She thought for sure she was going to faint with relief when Paul cooperated, handing her his **keys** and sweater. To keep from fainting, she temporarily steadied herself by holding on to the side table and wall while she caught her breath as he walked into the kitchen.

Once she had recovered, she hurried to join him, hoping to keep him distracted from thinking about his **keys**. While he poured the lemonade, she reached into the refrigerator for the relish plate she had put together earlier. "I hope you like fresh cut-up vegetables and dip for an appetizer to begin our barbeque," she said, opening a kitchen drawer to pull out a spoon, placing it into the dip. Walking to a cupboard, she reached for a bowl, opened the bag of potato chips that was **rest**ing on the sink, and emptied them into the bowl. Grabbing a chip and some dip, she said, "There's nothing like an evening barbeque to end a perfect day, wouldn't you agree, Paul?"

"Absolutely," Paul agreed grabbing a handful of chips and dipping them into the sour cream mix. "I probably should go and light the barbeque if you want to eat in the next half hour or so."

"I'm ready whenever you are." She opened another cupboard and handed him a box of matches while following him out her sliding door to the backyard.

"It's such a lovely evening, I thought it would be nice to eat outside. Are you warm enough to do that, Paul?"

"I think that's a great idea, and if it gets too cold, I did bring my sweater."

"Well, if you'll excuse me for a moment, Paul, I need to use the ladies' room, and I'll be back shortly." She saw him nod his head in agreement, being preoccupied with studying her barbeque setup. She was relieved he wasn't watching her because she was sure she had set a new speed record racing back into her house to grab his **keys** so she could make a copy. Earlier in the day she had rolled out the modeling clay into a round circle with her rolling pin. She even went so far as to take a ruler and **measure** the width to ensure its perfection. Once the clay met her specifications, she cut it in half.

Grabbing the precut clay from her bedroom drawer, she hurried and locked the bathroom door and began studying Paul's **keys**, looking for the **key** that had a red mark on it. She had paid careful attention to which **key** Paul had used this past week when they went on their walks so she would be prepared. Picking up the **key** with the red mark, she gently pressed one side of the **key** into the clay, making it flush to the clay. With great precision, she repeated the other half of the clay with the opposite side of the **key**. Last, but not least, the crucial step was to line up the two half's of the clay, perfection being a must, and lightly apply pressure around the edges of the **key** imprint in the clay to where it matched the same thickness as the original **key**. Mildred worried about making a mistake, so she decided she better make two impressions just in case one wasn't perfect; after all, she wasn't a professional locksmith. Now that she had completed both molds, she cautiously placed each in a protective box and used a moist rag to wipe Paul's **key** clean of any excess clay.

At this point, her heart was **beating** so violently, she was sure she would have a heart attack before ever delivering the **key** to the locksmith. She looked at her reflection in the mirror and was shocked at how pale her complexion was. Troubled by her appearance, she knew she better pull herself together or Paul would get suspicious. Adding some more blush to her cheeks, as well as refreshing her lipstick, she surveyed the room to make sure everything was in order before she left the area. Opening the door as **silently** as possible, she **listened** for Paul's whereabouts and then proceeded to tiptoe to her bedroom, placing the two boxes in a dresser drawer, and then she warily walked out to the side table where she quietly deposited his **keys**. Running her fingers lightly through her hair, she put on a pleasant smile and entered the kitchen.

Paul was just walking into the kitchen and announced he was ready to barbeque the main course if she had the meat ready.

"Perfect timing, Paul. Let me get the steaks out of the refrigerator for you. I like mine cooked medium. It won't take me long to finish setting the table, and then we can enjoy our meal." Mildred hoped she would be able to make it through the night without getting a migraine; to tell the truth, she was surprised she didn't already have one!

Rita had tried without success to reach Angie all night so she could question her on why Ted would be holding Debra's hand if she really had made the phone call to Debra that would have hopefully finished any trust between them. She doubted that Angie was even speaking to her, especially when she had ended their last conversation by slamming the phone down. While she sat stewing about the situation and wondering what to do to get back into Angie's good graces, she remembered Angie's weakness for clothes and how she could get another favor out of her. The question was, did she really want to put up with any more of Angie's temper tantrums? Time would tell, depending on how desperate things got.

Chapter 10

August had slipped into September, and September had arrived with its cooler temperatures, and the leaves began their spiraling descent to the ground while turning shades of russet brown and golden yellow to variations of carroty orange and red. The lunch bell had just rung, and since it was a beautiful fall day, Debra picked up her lunch tray from the cafeteria and followed her friends outside to eat. Everyone was talking about the upcoming fall carnival and dance, with activities of pumpkin carving and sack races to bobbing for apples and face painting.

"The bobbing for apples booth is being sponsored by the football team to help raise money for their equipment next year," Patty informed them. "I have volunteered to help in their booth, and anyone else that's interested, is welcome."

"It all **sounds** fun," Marsha responded.

"Does anyone know when the dance is going to be?" Becky asked.

"I think Mike was saying sometime in October, and it's going to have a theme called Oktoberfest," Patty replied.

"I wish it was a girl's choice dance, then I would have a chance of going," Charlotte stated with a pout.

"You never know what can happen, Charlotte! Look at Debra. She never thought she would meet a cool guy like Matt! Now they're quite the item, and if she's lucky, he may even ask her to the dance," Patty interjected.

Debra blushed and gave Patty a look that **silenced** anyone else from commenting. "Let's not jump to conclusions, Patty. You never know, Matt might meet someone 'pertier' than me between now and then! Charlotte, if you don't get asked, why don't you just ask someone to the dance? Most guys are afraid to ask because they don't want to be rejected."

"Well…I never thought about it that way. Maybe I will."

"Anyway, as I was saying, I could use some help with the apple-bobbing booth," Patty reminded them.

"What day in October is all this happening?" Marsha asked.

Pulling her small calendar out of her purse, Patty replied, "It's the last Saturday in October, just a few days before Halloween. The carnival is being held from noon until four in the afternoon, and the dance will be that night from seven until ten. It's going to be a lot of fun, and you'll be sorry if you miss it."

"It does **sound** like fun. Before I make any commitments, I'll have to check with my mom to see if I can be available," Marsha replied.

The others murmured they would have to do the same while they began gathering up their things in order to return to class. "As you get more details, keep us posted so we can be a part of the festivities, Patty," Debra replied. While walking to class, Debra thought about inviting Ted to the carnival and dance—that is, if Rita and Angela stopped interfering in their lives.

Mildred walked out of the locksmith with a look of pure relief and elation on her face, along with a brand-new **key** on her **key**-chain. She was also fighting the start of a migraine from the locksmith telling her the first mold she had made had not been successful. She could still feel the pounding of her heart, fearing the worst as he checked her second mold. Fortunately for her, everything had matched, and he was able to make a **key** from it. There was no way she was going to repeat the process of having to obtain his **key** again; once was bad enough! She wished that she didn't have to call Rita, however, at least she could report that she had completed phase two and was now ready to move onto phase three.

Debra was **practicing** the **piano** when she heard the telephone ring and her mother called her to the phone. She dreaded answering it, fearing it might be Angela with another story about Ted betraying her. "Hello," she answered timidly.

"Hi, Debra! This is Ted. Are you okay? You **sound** different."

"Oh hi, Ted! I'm so relieved it's you! Yes, I'm doing fine. I was **practicing** the **piano** and was just worried when I heard the phone ring that it might be Angela with another made-up story!"

"I've been doing a lot of thinking about that, and I wanted to apologize for being upset and giving you the **silent** treatment the other day. I know you were a victim, just like I was, and instead of being understanding, I got mad and took it out on you. I hope you'll forgive me."

"Oh, Ted, I was never mad at you. I was just frustrated that I believed someone else's lies. I'm sorry too. How's everything going for you this week?"

"I'm having a pretty good week. Started my new classes and so far, so good. I have a lot of homework and needed a break, so I wanted to call so I could hear your **voice**."

"Oh, Ted, that was just what I needed to hear you say. I love hearing your **voice** too! The one thing we have in common right now is we're both spending a lot of time doing homework! Do you have a favorite class?"

"Yes, I signed up for a **voice training** class and am doing some one-on-one **training** with a top **tenor** in the Orange County area. He has given me some great tips and has introduced me to a variety of new **songs**. I'm very excited about the **range** of experience it is giving me in helping to expand my **repertoire**."

"That **sounds** fantastic, Ted. I'm anxious to hear you **sing** some of your new **songs**."

"We should be having another **recital** coming up at the **conservatory** soon, and then you'll get to hear some of the **songs** I'm working on."

"You're right, and that's one of the reasons I thought I better start squeezing some extra **practice** time in so I'll be ready to **perform** too. I miss summer, where all I had to worry about was watering my grandfather's yard and **practicing** the **piano**. Those were the good ole days, wouldn't you agree?"

"Definitely! I'm glad you were home, Debra. I miss you, and I can't wait for the weekend to get here so we can spend a few hours together. You take care of yourself, and I'll see you soon, okay?"

"I can't wait, Ted. Thanks so much for calling. It made my week! Just a few more days and we'll be together. Take care!"

"Now, Mildred, I want you to test that **key** you had made and make sure it works. At this stage of the game, we can't have anything go wrong, and the last thing we need is to find out that **key** won't work!"

"Rita, that's going to be next to impossible for me to test out. What if Paul were to see me trying to unlock his door? How on earth would I explain that?"

"That's your problem, Mildred, and I expect you to deal with it! We have come too far to turn back now, and only perfection will do. I don't care what you have to do, Mildred. You just make it happen, you got it?"

It's a good thing Rita wasn't standing in front of her because Mildred might have whacked her in the head with her phone. She had had all she could take from Miss High and Mighty and was about ready to tell her what she could do with all her demands. Ending the phone conversation as soon as she could, she walked to her medicine cabinet to get some more pain pills to help soothe her aching head. Just a few more weeks and things would be taken care of, and then she would be on vacation with Paul where she could relax.

Debra had just settled herself into the **music** mobile and was excited about seeing Ted. The **rest** of her school week had gone well, and she was looking forward to **playing** her new **piece** for Brenda and enjoying the beautiful fall day.

"Greetings, **Middle C**, how's it going?" Ted asked after climbing into the **music** mobile.

"**Sounds** like you're in an **affabile** mood today, Ted," **Middle C** responded.

"Hello, gorgeous, how's my girl?" Ted asked, reaching over to give her a hug.

"I'm great now that you're here!" They shared a kiss and a special hug, and it felt wonderful to be back in his arms. "I've really missed you, Ted, and it's so nice to have this time together. We were so spoiled seeing each other so much in the summer that it's made going back to school a little more challenging, wouldn't you agree?"

"Absolutely. I think it helps now that we're both back in school and staying busy because it'll help the time go by quicker, at least I sure hope it will," Ted said while leaning over to give her another kiss. They were jolted apart by their landing at the **conservatory**, and they began laughing as they held hands and hurried to get to class.

"Welcome, students, I hope you're all doing well and have been able to keep pursuing your **musical** ambitions, as well as continuing with your school responsibilities at this busy time of year. Your instructors have informed me that you are all working on another **recital performance** and should be ready to **perform** again within a month's time. I am certainly looking forward to that time and will now excuse you to go to your classes."

Rita continued to be baffled over Ted's infatuation with the backward country bumpkin, and it angered her to see them holding hands as they walked to class. *Well, enjoy it while you can, because it's not going to last*, she cackled to herself.

Debra couldn't remember the last time she had enjoyed a Saturday as much as this one. Brenda was thrilled with the progress she was making on her **recital piece**, and she and Ted were getting along perfectly. She had mentioned the fall carnival and dance, and he seemed excited about reserving the time to be with her. Even **Middle C** had noticed how happy she was, and it made her want to skip up the stairs to begin her housecleaning for her grandfather.

She remembered her grandfather's request last week to mop the kitchen floor and did that first so it would have time to dry while she changed his sheets and cleaned the bathrooms. After emptying the trash and bringing up the last batch of clean clothes, she heard the front door open, then Mildred and her grandfather's **voices**. She was having such a great day that even seeing Mildred wasn't going to ruin it for her.

"Hello, Grandpa and Mildred! I hope you're enjoying your Saturday," she greeted them.

"Oh, indeed we are," Mildred replied. "We were just discussing our little vacation we're planning to go on next week, weren't we, Paul dear?" she asked smugly.

Debra noticed her grandfather cringe slightly when Mildred let the cat out of the bag. "You're going on a vacation next week?" Debra asked curiously.

"Yes, with our church group," her grandfather replied. "I was hoping that you could water my grass for me next Saturday when you're here cleaning. With the cooler weather, I'm sure it will only need to be watered on Saturday."

"Of course, Grandpa, I'd be happy to do that for you. When are you leaving and coming back?"

"We leave early next Thursday morning, and we will be gone for a week and two days, returning two weeks from this Saturday."

"I see. Well, I hope you have a wonderful time. I'm going to go and fold these clothes, and then I'll be finished, Grandpa."

"Thank you, Debra, I'll have your money ready for you when you're ready to leave."

It was hard not to let the news of her grandfather and Mildred's upcoming vacation dampen her spirits. *If Grandpa wants to ruin his life spending it with Mildred, then that's his business. I've certainly done everything I can to warn him!*

When she walked into the kitchen after arriving home, her mother could tell immediately something was wrong. "Did everything go okay at Grandpa's today, Debra?"

"Yes, I was having the best day ever, then Mildred waltzed into the house announcing she and Grandpa are going on vacation together next week."

"Really? Where are they going?"

"I didn't bother to ask. Does it really matter? All I can say is I've tried to warn him about Mildred, and he's too blind to realize what he's getting in to."

"I can see that this has really upset you, Debra. I wish I could say something to make you feel better. All I can say is I'm sorry it's so upsetting."

"I don't want him to get hurt, and I'm so afraid Mildred is just bad news!"

Chapter 11

Mildred hung up the phone and crossed another item off of her to-do list. She had just confirmed once again with the Salvation Army that they would meet her on Thursday at noon at Paul's home to pick up the old **player piano**. With all the critical factors coming to a **finale** this week, it was next to impossible to look forward to her vacation with Paul and even get excited about packing the new clothes she had recently purchased. She was beginning to wonder if she was doing the right thing. She knew she was too deeply involved to back out, and if Rita had her way, she'd be six feet under if she didn't follow through. She couldn't help wondering if there was a way out and what would happen if Paul ever found out what she had done. She couldn't think about that now. She just needed to stay focused on what she had to do.

Debra and her friends stayed after school on Tuesday afternoon for a meeting to discuss plans for the fall carnival. She was surprised when she saw Matt walk into the room and take a seat close by. "Well, if it isn't my favorite Strawberry! How y'all doin'?"

"We're all doin' great! How are you, Matt?" Debra asked while chuckling.

"Oh…you know me, I'm always doin' perty good. I'm happy to see you at this planning meeting. That means you're planning on going to the carnival and dance, right?"

Debra's heart skipped a **beat**, remembering she had asked Ted to go. He hadn't given her a definite answer yet, but she had pretty much already obligated herself to going with him. "Yes, I suppose it does mean I'm going, unless a last-minute conflict prevents me from going."

Fortunately for her, the meeting began, and everyone's attention was diverted to the person **conducting** the meeting.

By the time the planning meeting was over, everyone was excited about what was going to happen, and Debra decided to be vague about her own plans if Matt questioned her until she knew if Ted was going to be able to come. Patty was in a hurry to get going after the meeting, so she didn't have a chance to talk to Matt and just managed to wave at him as she quickly followed Patty and their friends out the door.

Rita was becoming more and more annoyed with Mildred's attitude and was beginning to have second thoughts about whether she could count on her to follow through on her commitment to their plan. Why were people being so flaky? Why couldn't they be like her? Come to think of it, she still hadn't been able to get Angie to answer her phone calls. What was this world coming to anyway? All she could do was hope and wait to see if Mildred would keep her end of the bargain.

Mildred didn't sleep a wink all night worrying about what she had to do today. She checked her watch for the umpteenth time that morning wishing the five o'clock hour would arrive. Pacing back and forth across her bedroom floor didn't make the time go by any faster. Finally her grandfather clock began its five o'clock chime and when it finished she would give Paul a phone call.

"Hello, Paul, this is Mildred."

"Hello, Mildred, what's wrong? You **sound** a little under the weather."

"Oh, Paul, you're not going to believe it. I woke up with one of my migraines this morning, and I'm not going to be able to join you this morning as planned. I called Brother Wilson, and he advised me that I can book another flight that will meet up with everyone by Friday night. I didn't want you to get to our meeting place and wonder where I was."

"I'm sorry to hear you're not feeling well, Mildred. I'd be happy to wait and go with you when you get feeling better."

Mildred began to panic, never even entertaining the idea that he wouldn't go ahead without her. "Oh, Paul, I couldn't ask you to do that. You must go ahead. I would feel terrible if I ruined this trip for you. Promise me you'll go as originally planned. Trust me, I will catch up to you...okay, Paul, dear?"

"Well...if you insist, Mildred. However, I really don't mind waiting."

"Promise me you'll go, Paul. I just couldn't live with myself if I caused you to miss out on anything. I know I will **rest** a lot better and will get over this ridiculous migraine if I'm not worrying about you."

"Okay, Mildred, I'll go ahead as planned and will look forward to seeing you in a day or so. Thanks for letting me know. You take care of yourself."

When Mildred hung up the phone, she was sure if her migraines didn't kill her, she would die of a heart attack for sure. She was definitely not cut out for all this sneaky, underhanded stuff. She didn't even have a migraine but felt like one was coming on just trying to keep up with her end of phase three!

Mildred continued to worry all morning about what would happen if Paul decided not to go on the trip as planned and she got caught letting the Salvation Army into his home to take away his **player piano**. She checked the time, and it was a little after eight in the morning. If Paul had left as scheduled, his home would have been vacant now for well over two hours. She quickly dialed his phone number and breathed a huge sigh of relief when it just kept ringing. Feeling much better about the situation, she decided to get dressed and go over to Paul's home just before eleven. That would give her time to see if the **key** she had made would open his door.

Mildred drove past Paul's home to be sure once more that he wasn't home. Not seeing a single car around, she decided it would be best to park her car a half a block away and walk to his home just in case someone might recognize her car being parked out front. As she carefully climbed the stairs, she thought her heart was going to jump out of her chest from absolute fright. If that wasn't bad enough, her fingers shook from sheer panic while trying to insert the **key** she had made. Breathing deeply to try to steady her shaking fingers seemed next to impossible as she cautiously inserted the **key** into Paul's lock. So far, so good, but, when she turned the **key**, nothing happened.

Oh, this can't be happening to me, Mildred mourned.

Looking at the **key**, she realized she had put the wrong **key** into the lock, and she uttered some curse words describing her stupidity while inserting the correct **key**. This time when she turned the **key**, she felt the bolt cooperate, and the door unlocked, allowing her to turn the knob and gain entry into Paul's home.

The Salvation Army had finally removed the **player piano** out of the basement and were loading it into their truck when Dale happened to drive by Mr. Herman's house on his way back to Highland High School after taking his lunch break.

"That's strange," Dale mumbled as he stared at the men loading the large **piano** into their truck. "Mr. Herman never mentioned he was donating a **piano** to the Salvation Army. The next time I see him, I'll have to ask him about it."

Mildred thought they would never leave and could barely stand up from the pounding in her head. "Are you men about finished? I have a million other things I need to do today."

"Sorry, ma'am, the **player piano** was a lot heavier than we anticipated. If we had known it was this heavy, we would have put in a request for one more man to help. We almost canceled moving it when we first began lifting it but decided to give it one more try."

"Well, be that as it may, I have things to do and places to go and can't waste any more time with the likes of you."

"Here's your receipt, and we appreciate your donation. Have a good day."

"I will once you're out of my hair," Mildred mumbled as she hurried to close Paul's garage. She went downstairs to turn the lights off in the **music** room and couldn't get over how bare the room was without the **player piano**.

"Good riddance to bad rubbish is all I have to say about it."

She closed the door and went back upstairs to the kitchen, where she collected her purse off of the kitchen table. She looked carefully around the room to make sure she hadn't left any evidence that she had been in the room. Hurrying over to the living room windows, she looked out to see if anyone was around and finding all clear, went out the front door and quickly locked it. Her legs were wobbling and shaking as she made her way down the stairs, and she prayed she could keep herself together until she managed to hobble back to her car.

After settling into the front seat, she grabbed the steering wheel to steady herself and continued to breathe deeply while gaining control over her shaking body. One thing was definite, she would never do anything like this again. She decided once she got home, she would take a dose of migraine headache medicine and crawl into bed and sleep until she couldn't sleep anymore, and if Rita called, she would just have to wait until she was **rest**ed enough to talk to her!

Debra couldn't believe it was Friday already and was looking forward to the last football game of the season, as well as the weekend. She knew her grandfather would be on vacation with Mildred, and the only good thing about that was she didn't have to worry about running into her. She had to admit she was kind of excited about watering his yard because it brought back a little nostalgia, reminding her of recent summer days spent with Ted.

Debra and Patty were lucky enough to find front-row seats to the afternoon football game and loved sitting so close to the football players. Patty was especially on cloud nine and constantly shouted words of encouragement to Mike. The final game of the season was with Highland High School, and for a few minutes Debra scanned the opposite bleachers to see if Dale was attending the game. She sighed with relief, remembering their initial encounter and his crush on her. She was grateful he had moved on to pursue someone else.

The game was very competitive, with each team fighting hard to win the last game; however, Skyline was victorious once more, scoring the winning touchdown. Debra looked at Patty and thought it was a good thing Skyline won their last game or being around Patty was not going to be fun. They drove over to Hardy's after the game, and Debra was surprised and a little disappointed not to see Matt. For a second, she wondered if he had found another girlfriend and had mixed emotions about it. Dismissing it from her mind, she soon mingled with other friends and had an enjoyable night.

Rita had just hung up the phone after talking to Mildred. She had a very smug look on her face and couldn't help the wicked laugh that came tumbling out of her mouth while she enjoyed the scene in her mind of Debra going downstairs and opening her grandfather's **music** room to find the **player piano** gone! Oh, how she wished she could be there to see that!

"Serves her right to try to compete with me! Move over, you little country bumpkin! The big city girl has moved in to claim what's rightfully hers!"

Chapter 12

"I'll be home a little later than usual, Mom. Remember, Grandpa needs me to water his lawn today."

"I'm glad you reminded me of that. I had forgotten. I wonder how he's doing on his little vacation with Mildred."

"I don't know, and I don't really care. I've tried to warn him, but he's too lovesick to **listen** to me," Debra replied in frustration.

"Try not to be so hard on him, dear. We don't understand how lonely he's been and what he has gone through since Grandma passed away."

"You're right, Mom. I'm sorry. I just get angry because I don't want to see him get hurt."

"You and me both, honey. Well, you get going, and I hope you have an enjoyable morning."

Debra turned on the radio after starting the car and was excited to hear a **song** that reminded her of Ted. She rolled the car window down and loved the feel of the cool, crisp fall air as it blew her hair while driving. With fall arriving, she looked forward to all the fun activities that came with it, and she hoped Ted would have an answer on whether he could attend the fall carnival and dance with her.

After arriving at her grandfather's home, she hurried outside and started the first water station and then went back inside to set the timer. She checked her appearance in the mirror and reached into her bag for her perfume. While going downstairs, she pinched her cheeks to make sure they had a healthy glow and then hurried to open the **music** room door. She didn't know why, but something just felt different today. Carefully turning on the lights, she paused as she surveyed the room. It seemed larger than usual, and she couldn't figure out why until she saw the bare wall where the old **player piano** used to be. Doing a quick double take, she couldn't believe what she was seeing!

"Where's Grandpa's **player piano**?" she asked in a **voice** filled with panic. "Oh no…this can't be happening." She ran over to the spot where it used to be and walked back and forth, frantically begging it to reappear while she continued to look for a clue as to its whereabouts.

She wanted to tell someone but knew Ted wouldn't be home. She had no way to contact her grandfather or even **Middle C**.

"Oh no, I'm going to miss my class today at the **conservatory**!"

She thought about calling her mother, but then she would have to explain the whole situation with **Middle C** and the **conservatory**. What was going on? Did Mildred and Rita do this? Wow…if they did, she had totally underestimated their capabilities. They were more powerful than she had ever imagined or given them credit for!

"Hello, **Middle C**," Ted greeted as he entered the **music** mobile. He looked down the aisle to where Debra normally sat and didn't see her. Surprised, he asked, "Where's Debra today?"

"I'm not sure. She didn't summon me today like she normally does. Did she say anything to you about not attending class today?"

"No, not a word," Ted said thoughtfully. "I hope everything's okay. It would be nice if we had a portable phone to call and check on her. Remind me to invent one someday. It would come in very handy, wouldn't it?"

"I should say so, Ted, very handy indeed."

Rita looked up to see Ted walk into the **conservatory** by himself, and she could hardly contain her joy and laughter when she realized it was because the poor little bumpkin didn't have her **player piano** so she couldn't summon her **mediator**! Yes, her plan was working, and she was enjoying every minute of it!'

Mildred had flown in late Friday evening and had taken a taxi to join the church group at the hotel they were staying in. Now that her part of the plan was completed, she could try to relax and enjoy her vacation time with Paul, and when they returned home and he found out about his missing **player piano**, she would have the perfect alibi to cover up her part in its disappearance. After checking in and getting settled in her room, she went right to bed so she would be refreshed in the morning.

Mildred got up early and took great care in getting dressed for the day. She needed to be at her absolute best so Paul wouldn't have any doubts about what she had really been up to. After getting directions to the dining room from the front desk attendant, it didn't take her long to spot Paul in the room.

"Hello, Mildred, how are you feeling?" Paul said as he stood to greet her.

"I am feeling back to my healthy self again. I went in for a quick checkup, and my doctor switched my medication, and I have never felt better. I'm ready for some fun and can't wait to start participating with our group."

Debra had just arrived home after spending a marathon day of watering and cleaning her grandfather's house. "Mom, you're not going to believe what happened at Grandpa's house."

"What happened?" her mother quickly asked.

"When I went downstairs to start Grandpa's laundry, the **music** room seemed different, like it was larger than usual. When I looked around the room, I saw that his **player piano** was gone. Did he tell you he was getting rid of it?"

"No, he didn't, and I have to say, I don't think he would ever get rid of it. I know how much he loves that **piano**."

"What could have happened to it?"

"That is a very good question, and one I wish Grandpa was here to answer. He's not going to be back from his vacation for another week or so, and I'm not sure what his itinerary is so I can't contact him to ask."

The telephone rang, interrupting their conversation. "Debra, the phone's for you," Linda called from downstairs.

"I'm going to take that downstairs…okay, Mom?"

"Of course, dear," her mother replied, lost in her own thoughts.

"Hello," Debra replied into the telephone.

"Debra, it's Ted. Where were you today? I really missed you?"

"Oh, Ted, I'm so glad it's you," Debra hurried to inform him while pulling on the phone cord, stretching it to reach into her room where she could close the door and talk to him privately. "When I went downstairs to summon **Middle C**, my grandfather's **player piano** was gone!"

"What do you mean it was gone?" Ted asked confused.

"It's not in his house anymore. It's missing. When I opened the **music** room door, I thought something seemed different, and as I looked around the room, the wall where the **player piano** normally sits was empty!"

"Wow…I don't even know what to say. Where's your grandpa?"

"He's on that stupid vacation with Mildred."

"Do you think Mildred had something to do with it?" Ted asked.

"I would like to say yes, but she went on that vacation with him, so I'm not sure what to think."

"This is soooo strange. Do you think Rita did it?"

"How could she do it? She doesn't have a **key** to my grandfather's house or know his schedule. A big part of me wants to say they both did it, but I'm not sure how they did it!"

"This whole thing is unbelievable!"

"I know! How am I supposed to get **Middle C** to pick me up now?"

"I'll get in touch with **Middle C** and fill him in on what's happened and see what he wants to do, and then I'll call and let you know."

"Thanks, Ted. Needless to say, it has been a long, horrible day. I'm so glad you called so I could tell you what happened."

"I was telling **Middle C** today that I wish I could invent a portable phone because we didn't know if something had happened to you and we didn't have a way to call you."

"I wish you had a portable phone too. That's an amazing idea. You should really look into that!"

"Well, the important thing is you're okay. Now we just have to find out what happened to your grandfather's **player piano**. I'll get in touch with **Middle C** and then let you know what he says. I missed you today, Debra, and was worried about you all day."

"I missed you too, Ted. Thanks so much for calling me, and I'll be anxious to know what **Middle C** tells you."

Mildred and Paul's church group were vacationing in Clay, West Virginia, where they were enjoying the annual apple festival. Brother Wilson had informed the group that Clay was the birthplace of the golden delicious apple and that it was also West Virginia's official state fruit. They were having the festival kickoff that day beginning at two, and it would continue for a week, with highlights featuring apple vendors, entertainment, antique car shows, a parade, apple-baking contests, a quilt show, as well as a variety of other vendors featuring their crafts and food.

"I'm sure looking forward to tasting all the apple-baked goods for the apple contest," Paul said, licking his lips in anticipation.

"I want to find the vendor who makes apple dolls. I hear they are out of this world," Mildred replied with enthusiasm.

Finishing their breakfast, they agreed to meet back at the bus in a half an hour.

Debra was working on the Martins' ironing when the phone rang. She was happy when it was for her and hoped it was Ted with an update.

"Hi, Debra! I got ahold of **Middle C** and told him the latest, and he was shocked and concerned! He's not sure who made the **player piano** disappear, but he's pretty sure Mildred or Rita had something to do with it. Do you remember seeing an old **pipe organ** in your grandfather's **music** room?"

"Yes, it's on the west wall," Debra advised.

"Oh good. Well, **Middle C** said you could summon him on that. Just turn it on and **play** the **middle C key** three times and it should **transpose** him there."

"That is great news, Ted! I will definitely try that next Saturday when I go over to clean and water. He and Mildred aren't supposed to be back until late Saturday night. I was so upset by his missing **player piano** I didn't get a chance to ask you about your class or going to the **conservatory** today."

"Everything went well with the exception of missing you like crazy. Mr. Walker said he would like our next **performance** to be sometime in the middle to the end of October. Hopefully that will give everyone enough time to be prepared."

"Speaking of October, Ted, did you get a chance to check to see if you can go to my fall carnival and dance?"

"No, not yet. The manager that does the scheduling said that's too far out for him to make a final commitment on. I'm sorry, Debra. For some reason, the stars aren't lining up for us, are they?"

"They definitely didn't line up today, did they? I don't want to start thinking negatively, though, because then we'll be sunk for sure. Did you happen to notice Rita's face when you walked into the **conservatory** without me today?"

"No, I didn't. I was totally preoccupied with worrying about what happened to you. I wish I would have thought about that. Her face might have given a huge clue as to what happened to the disappearance of your grandfather's **player piano**."

"Well, don't **beat** yourself up about it, Ted. You know what they say about hindsight. Going forward, we really have to pay attention to our surroundings and anything that might seem off."

"I will, Debra, and I want you to be especially careful. Even though Mildred is out of town, I don't trust Rita. You mean the world to me, and I don't know what I'd do if I lost you."

"Thanks, Ted, it makes me feel good to know how much you care. You be careful too. Who knows what Rita and Angela have in store for you as well."

"I hate to go, but I've gotta get ready for my Olive Garden shift. Be safe, my love."

"You too. Bye for now."

Chapter 13

Mildred was having the time of her life on vacation with Paul and soon forgot about getting rid of his **player piano** until they stopped by a vendor's booth who sold **ragtime music rolls** for **player pianos**. The vendor had his own **player piano** sitting in the booth, set on auto **play**, and it continuously **played catchy music tunes**. As hard as she tried to divert Paul's attention, he had every intention of stopping at the dreaded booth. While **listening** to Paul go on and on about his beloved **player piano**, she thought she was going to be sick, and she nearly lost it when he purchased a half dozen **music rolls**, stating he could hardly wait to get home to **play** them on his **piano**. Boy, would she be in trouble if he ever found out it was her that got rid of his beloved **player piano**!

"What's the matter, Mildred? You're looking a little peaked?" Paul asked.

"Oh…I think it's this humidity. I'm not quite used to it. Maybe we could sit in the shade for a few minutes, and it'll pass."

"That's a good idea. You go grab a table for us while I go get some lemonade."

Up to this point, Mildred had been on cloud nine, but now her world was slowly starting to crumble as the truth began its gradual crawl to catch up to her. She decided she better pull herself together quickly or Paul would begin to get suspicious of her behavior, which could then **lead** him to finding out just how devious she was!

Surprisingly the school week was going by a lot quicker than Debra had anticipated, and she was looking forward to the weekend so she could try summoning **Middle C** by using the old **pipe organ**. School had just ended for the day, and she and Patty were going to attend a carnival planning meeting. When they walked into the classroom, she immediately saw Matt, who waved, and she couldn't help wishing she knew if Ted was going to be able to attend or not. Returning his wave, they headed in his direction and took a seat.

"Well, hello to two of the pertiest girls in the school," Matt replied cheerfully.

"Hello to you too, good looking," Patty immediately responded.

Debra returned his smile but didn't say anything.

"Cat got your tongue today, Strawberry?"

"No," she replied shyly.

"What…you don't think I'm good looking?" Matt teased.

"Of course I do, but I'm not going to say it. If I did, your head wouldn't fit into your Texas cowboy hat!"

"Ouch! You're in a feisty mood today, aren't you, Strawberry girl?"

Thank heavens the meeting started, and she looked at Matt and shook her head in reply to his question. He responded with a wink, and she thought she better turn her attention to the guy in charge before she got herself into trouble. At the end of the meeting, several assignments had been made; Debra had volunteered to make a poster, listing who would be in charge and at what time they would be scheduled to work; Patty had volunteered to purchase apples and to bring a large container that could be used to hold the apples while people bobbed for them; and Matt had volunteered to fill the containers with water and to help monitor the water levels throughout the day. There were, of course, others at the meeting who would assist the three with their assignments.

Debra was relieved that Matt was in a hurry to leave after the meeting and didn't have time to ask her any more questions about her plans for attending the carnival or dance. Hopefully Ted would have an answer by the weekend.

"Do you think you'll go to the carnival and dance with Matt?" Patty asked.

"I'm not sure yet. I've asked Ted if he can go, and he's waiting for his work to let him know if he can get the time off," Debra replied. "Do you think Matt will ask me?"

"From what I could see before our meeting, he's still got the hots for you," Patty said with a mischievous smile.

"I never thought I'd see the day that I was juggling two guys! I could definitely see you doing that, but certainly not me, Patty! This isn't fun!"

"Oh yeah, sure, that's what they all say," Patty teased back.

"Has Mike asked you to go?"

"He certainly has. Otherwise, I wouldn't have volunteered for any of this bobbing for apples stuff!"

"Okay, just checking to make sure," Debra said. They pulled up in front of her house, and Debra waved and thanked her for the ride.

Debra woke up before her alarm went off Saturday morning, anxious to get over to her grandfather's home so she could summon **Middle C** using the **pipe organ**. She got into the shower, wanting to wash her hair so she would look extra nice for Ted since they hadn't seen each other for a few weeks.

"Why are you up so early, Miss Debra, on a Saturday morning?" her mother asked when she walked into the kitchen.

"I guess I'm just used to getting up early during the week, and I woke up early. It's okay. I have a lot to do today with the watering and cleaning, and then I need to get home so I can pick up the Martins' ironing. By the time I finish all of that, there's barely enough free time left for me, you know?"

"I hadn't thought about it that way, but it makes sense. Are you going to have some breakfast?"

"I thought I would grab an apple and a peach. I'm not very hungry. I'm sure Grandpa has some bread, so if I get hungry, I'll just fix some toast. Is that okay?"

"Yes, that'll work. You take care, honey."

"I will. Bye, Mom."

It was another crisp fall morning, and Debra enjoyed her drive over to her grandfather's home. The leaves were definitely turning various shades of colors, and many had already began their journey to the ground. She locked her car and dashed up the steps to her grandfather's home. It didn't take long to start the watering, and soon she was on her way down to the **music** room.

After opening the door, she carefully walked over to the dusty old **pipe organ**. Before touching it, she looked over to the spot where the **player piano** used to be, wishing it had secretly made its way back. Still staring at the vacant spot, she decided to get some Kleenex out of the bathroom so she could wipe away some of the dust on the old **pipe organ**. Once it was clean, she found the switch and turned it on. While warming up, it sputtered a few times, and then very carefully, she located the **middle c key** and pushed it three times. Like magic, she heard the familiar **tune** and saw **notes** appearing all around the **organ** while twisting and spiraling into a circle until they delivered **Middle C**.

"Oh, Mr. **Middle C**, you don't know how good it is to see you," Debra cried as she ran forward to give him a hug.

"It certainly is a pleasure to see you again too, my dear girl. You gave Master Theodore and I quite a scare last week when neither one of us heard a word from you."

Turning to the bare wall where the **player piano** had formerly been, she said, "Well, as you can see, I wasn't exaggerating. The old **player piano** is really gone."

"Such a heartbreaking tragedy," murmured **Middle C** while shaking his head. "We will certainly get to the bottom of this, and I pity the person who committed this terrible deed. Come along now, Miss Debra, it is time we were on our way."

Debra thought they would never reach Ted, eager to see him. He must have felt the same way because he rushed aboard the **music** mobile to see if she was there. "Oh, Debra, it's so good to see you." He hurried down the aisle.

They hugged each other as if it had been years since they had seen each other rather than a few weeks. "It looks like you had success when you summoned **Middle C** on the **pipe organ** this morning."

"I don't think I could have taken another week of not seeing you, Ted."

"I know what you mean, Debra," he said while holding her closer.

"Today when we walk into the **conservatory**, let's both try to look as nonchalantly as possible at Rita to see if we can pick up any **vibes** from her," Debra suggested.

"I agree, and hopefully that witch will show her true colors, and we can get to the bottom of all this craziness."

They landed shortly at the **conservatory** and tried walking in as they normally did while studying Rita as discreetly as possible. They both noticed a slight visible flinch from her; she appeared shocked to see Debra.

Once seated Ted asked, "Did you see her flinch when she saw you?"

"Yes, I certainly did. She was definitely not expecting to see me, was she?"

"No. Now the tricky part is, how do we get her to tell us what she knows?"

Once again, they were interrupted by Mr. Walker bringing the group to order. Debra's mind was elsewhere, and she hoped Mr. Walker hadn't said anything too important because she had definitely missed hearing whatever he said. She did, however, notice that Rita was slow to leave the room and seemed to watch her every move.

"How did that country bumpkin get here?" Rita grumbled to herself. "I thought we had gotten rid of her ability to summon her **mediator**. Something's got to be done about that! Mildred, dear, you only thought your part was finished!"

On the way back from the **conservatory**, Ted asked **Middle C**, "Did you have a chance to talk to Rita's **mediator** to see if you could find anything out about the missing **player piano**?"

"I tried. However, he's staying very tight lipped. I can't tell if he knows anything or not. He's a strange one," **Middle C** informed them.

Debra remembered the fall carnival and asked Ted, "Did you find out if you're going to be able to come to my fall carnival and dance yet?"

"No, I wish I had an answer for you, but the guy who does the **scheduling** doesn't like us to bug him. I was afraid to ask him again in case he gave me a definite no."

"I understand, Ted. Sorry to keep bugging you about it."

"Is there someone you want to go with…other than me?" Ted asked.

"No, Ted, I just have to fill out a schedule for the bobbing for apples booth and wanted to make sure I don't schedule me to work at a time you would get there."

"Okay, I just wanted to make sure. Looks like we're here at my **rest** stop now." He leaned forward and kissed her and then walked down to exit the **music** mobile.

When **Middle C** delivered her back to her grandfather's **music** room, she was in deep thought.

"A penny for your thoughts, Miss Debra."

"Oh…I was just thinking about the disappearance of my grand-father's **player piano** and who could have done it. It's a big piece of furniture, you know. You can't just slip it into your pocket and take it. Someone must have seen something. The question is who?"

"I will keep my eyes and **ears** open as well! I feel positive we will get this all figured out."

"I sure hope so. My grandfather gets back from his vacation late tonight, and he's going to be devastated when he finds out about his missing **player piano**."

"Yes, I imagine he will," **Middle C** replied thoughtfully. "I will see you soon, dear girl. **Practice** diligently."

Paul and Mildred had just landed at the Salt Lake City Airport and were waiting to pick up their luggage. "That was one of the most enjoyable vacations I've been on in a long time," Paul stated. "I'm anxious to get home now and hang up my new apple hat I purchased for my souvenir wall in my **music** room, and while I'm hanging it up, I'll **play** one of the new **songs** I purchased for my **player piano**."

Mildred immediately panicked when she heard Paul's plans, and her head began to throb. Trying her best to cover up her alarm, she replied, "That **sounds** like a wonderful idea, Paul. I'm pretty tired tonight, and I hope you don't mind if I go straight home, but I would like to come over tomorrow and see where you've hung your hat and **listen** to your new **music**."

"Consider it a date, Mildred."

Chapter 14

After a good night's **rest**, Paul was anxious to get up, have break-fast, and go downstairs to his **music** room to decide where he would hang his new hat while **listening** to the new **piano rolls** with perforations he had purchased for his **player piano**. After cleaning up the kitchen, he began whistling the **tune** of the first **piano roll** he planned to **play** as he hurried downstairs, barely able to contain his excitement at what he was about to hear. When he opened the door and turned on the light, however, the **music** room felt different; he wasn't sure why. Looking around, he immediately saw the reason and couldn't believe his eyes. He was either having a terrible nightmare or this was the worst practical joke someone had ever **played** on him. Walking over to the spot where his beloved **player piano** had once sat, he couldn't believe it was now gone.

"When did this happen?" he said out **loud**. Not knowing what else to do, he ran upstairs to call his daughter.

"Hello, Jane, I hope I'm not calling too early."

"No, not at all. How was your vacation, Dad?"

"It was one of the best ones I've had. However, I have an urgent matter that has come up, and I need to talk to you about it. Do you have a few minutes?"

"Of course I do. What's wrong, Dad?"

"I think my **player piano** has been stolen. Did Debra say anything to you about it being gone from the basement?"

"Yes, she came home very upset a week ago Saturday and advised me that when she went down to do your wash, it was gone. Who on earth would do something like this?"

"That's just it, I can't think of anyone who would have done it—or for that matter, how on earth they did it without me knowing or anyone seeing it!"

"I am so sorry to hear about it, Dad, and I wish I had some answers on who and why, but I'm clueless as well."

"Okay, Jane. Thanks for letting me call so early. If I figure it out, I'll let you know."

"Okay, Dad. Take care."

Mildred didn't sleep very well, worrying about how Paul would react to his missing **player piano**. She had decided her best defense would be to get up early like she normally did and drive over to Paul's on the pretense of being excited to see where he was going to hang his new hat and act excited to **listen** to his new **music** for his **player piano**.

Ringing the doorbell, she inhaled deeply to try to calm her shaky nerves. "Good morning, Paul. I hope I didn't come over too early. I thought you'd be anxious to try out your new **music** on your **player piano**."

"Good morning, Mildred. Please forgive me, but I'm not in a very good mood this morning because someone stole my **piano**."

"You can't be serious, Paul, not your beautiful **baby grand piano**!"

"No, not that **piano**. My old **player piano** that I keep downstairs."

"But how can that be? I would imagine that **piano** is extremely heavy. Who would do that?"

"I don't know, but you can bet I will find out!"

Mildred had to work hard to control her trembling. She had no doubt that Paul wouldn't stop until he found out who the culprit was. She could only hope it remained a deep, dark secret.

Debra was busy with her school week; however, she still managed to squeeze in time to **practice**. She was a little concerned about whether or not she would be ready to **perform** in the next **recital** at the **conservatory**. She knew she would have the **song learned** by then, but she wasn't sure if she would have it committed to **memory**. Once again the telephone interrupted her **practice** time.

"Hello," Debra answered.

"Hello, Strawberry!"

"How's it going, Matt?"

"Great...now that I'm talking to you. I wanted to know if you would like to go out on a fun date Friday night with a group of friends to a corn maze. Have you ever gone to one of those before?"

"Yes, and you're right, it is a lot of fun. What time did you have in mind?"

"I could come and pick you up around six, and then we'll meet everyone at the corn maze, where we'll roast some hot dogs and then try not to get too lost in the maze. I'll bring you back home around eleven or so."

After checking with her parents, she let Matt know she had their permission to go.

"I am looking forward to spending another fun evening with you, Strawberry." They talked a few more minutes, and then she hung up.

"Matt seems like a very nice boy, Debra."

"Yes, he is. Did you know he calls me Strawberry?"

"I like that nickname. Do you like it, or does it bother you?"

"I like it! Has Grandpa said anymore about his **player piano**?"

"No, but I know he's very upset by that whole situation. No one can figure out how it got taken. Sooner or later something's bound to come up."

"Mildred, I am calling to see how things are going on your end?" Rita asked snappily.

"Everything is going as it should be going, Rita. Why do you ask?"

"Well, last Saturday Debra showed up for a class I have with her, and she always used the **player piano** to help **transpose** her way there. I was trying to figure out how she got to class if you really got rid of that **piano**."

"Are you trying to drive me crazy, Rita? If so, you are doing a good job of it! For your information, I was on vacation with her grandfather, and I haven't the slightest idea what she used. But I can tell you it wasn't that ridiculous old **player piano**! Now why don't you pick on someone else? I've had it up to my yin yang with you!" Mildred slammed the phone down and hoped Rita would get the message and leave her alone. Her phone continued to ring several more times; however, Mildred chose to ignore it.

"You think you can ignore me, Mildred? Well, we'll just see about that! I wonder how Paul would feel if he knew *you* were the one that made his precious **player piano** disappear." Rita's comment was followed by several minutes of her despicable laughter while contemplating what to do next about the bothersome Mildred.

"You two have fun at the corn maze," Mrs. Wilkin said to Debra and Matt as they left on their date. "I think Matt seems like a nice young man," she said to her husband.

"Yes, I agree, but I hate to see our girls growing up so fast."

When Debra and Matt arrived at the corn maze, they saw Patty and Mike, along with Connie and Anthony, waiting for them. After Matt paid their entry fee, they each picked up a barbeque stick, slid a hot dog onto the end, and hurried over to join their friends, who were roasting their dogs. "Look out, Anthony, your dog just caught on fire," Connie yelled while trying to suppress a giggle. Needless to say several more dogs caught on fire before the meal was cooked; however, they were all none for the worse when all was said and done!

The corn maze had several options to choose from; two of the **courses** already had records set on them, and people were encouraged to try to **beat** the record. When the record was **beat**en, you were eligible to win a prize. There were other mazes to choose from, and you could take your time going through them, hopefully finding your way out before closing time. The guys were adventurous and of **course**, wanted to see if they could break the current record times. The time to **beat** was ten minutes, so the girls decided to gab while the guys tried to prove their masculinity. Everyone was having a blast, and the girls hardly noticed when the boys came darting out of the maze with an exciting new record of nine minutes and forty-seven seconds, winning them each a free cotton candy! Picking up their prizes, they grabbed their girls, and spent the **rest** of the evening trying to find their way through the massive mazes.

That night as Debra slid into bed, she couldn't help smiling when she thought about the fun time she had had on her date with Matt. Snuggling down into her covers, she hoped her Saturday at her grandfather's would be a good day. She was excited to show him how she could summon **Middle C** using the **pipe organ**; however, she still felt sad over the loss of his **player piano**. She wished there was something she could do to bring back his **piano**, but for now, she was tired and it was getting harder and harder to keep her eyes open.

Morning came quickly, and soon she found herself on her grandfather's doorstep ringing the doorbell. "Good morning, Grandpa."

"Hello, my dear granddaughter, please come in," he said, holding the door open for her.

"Oh, Grandpa, I'm so sorry about your **player piano**. It must have been a huge shock for you."

"You can say that again! I think I'm still in shock."

"Do you have any idea who could have done this?" Debra asked.

"No, I don't know where to begin to look or who to ask. I'm not even sure if you can summon **Middle C** anymore."

"Well, I do have some good news. I am able to summon **Middle C**. Do you remember me telling you about the boy I met over the summer named Ted? He got in contact with **Middle C** and told him that your **player piano** had been stolen. **Middle C** gave Ted **instructions** on how I can summon him on your old **pipe organ**. I just turn it on and **play** the **middle c key** three times, and he appears."

"Is that right? Well, it's nice to know we can still stay in touch with him that way," Paul replied.

"Would it be okay if I go downstairs and summon him now? I have my class at the **conservatory**."

"You go right ahead. I'll leave a list of things to do on the kitchen table in case I'm not here when you get back."

Debra hurried to hug her grandfather and then went downstairs to the **music** room. "Any new information on the **player piano**?" **Middle C** asked when he appeared.

"No. My grandfather made it back from his vacation and was certainly shocked to see it gone. He can't figure it out either."

"Sooner or later, something or someone will shed some light on it. I just feel someone knows something about it. Should we be off now, dear girl?"

She watched as **Middle C** reached for his **metronome**, turning the dials so they could get going. It wasn't long until they arrived at Ted's **rest** stop. "Greetings, everyone, hope all is going well this morning," Ted announced as he stepped into the **music** mobile. "How's my Debra today?"

"I'm having a good day. It was hard seeing my grandfather so sad about his **player piano** this morning. **Middle C** seems to think something will turn up on it. We just have to be patient and wait. How are you doing?"

"I've had a good week. Work is going well, no unwanted visits from Rita and her friend, and school is going good. I'm keeping up on all of my homework."

They landed at the **conservatory**, and both agreed to keep a careful eye on Rita for any clues about her possible involvement with the missing **player piano**. To their disappointment, today she didn't even flinch when she saw them enter the classroom together. "So much for that," Ted murmured quietly to Debra.

Debra received positive feedback on the progress she was making on her latest **recital piece**. She promised to continue working on it and committed to the process of starting to **memorize** it.

Breaking the **silence** on the ride back from the **conservatory**, Ted said, "I plan on talking to the manager who makes the schedule this week to see if I can get the Saturday before Halloween off."

"Oh, that would be great. I'm going to keep my fingers crossed he'll give it to you," Debra said with a hopeful look.

"That makes two of us. All I can do is try, and hopefully fate will be on our side." They felt the **music** mobile jerk slightly when they landed, and Ted leaned forward to give Debra a warm, affectionate kiss. "Goodbye for now, my sweet!"

Debra landed at her grandfather's **music** room and waved goodbye to **Middle C** and headed upstairs. All was quiet after she opened the kitchen door, and she saw the list her grandfather had left, along with some money for her, sitting on the table. She quickly got busy with the chores while lost in thoughts about her day at the **conservatory** and her fun date at the maze the night before with Matt. While folding the last load of clean clothes, the doorbell rang, and Debra hurried to the door to see Dale through the peephole. She almost didn't open the door, wondering what he wanted.

"Hi, Debra, is your grandfather around?" Dale asked quickly.

"No, he's out, and I'm not sure when he'll be back. Is there something I can help you with?"

"No, not really," Dale said, debating about leaving, and then he changed his mind. "I was just surprised a week or so ago when I was on my lunch hour to see the Salvation Army picking up his **piano**."

"What did you say?" Debra said, coming to immediate attention.

"Well, I know how much he loves **music**, especially his **pianos**, and I thought he would give the **piano** to you before donating it to the Salvation Army."

"Are you sure you saw the Salvation Army here taking away the **piano**?" Debra asked in a very serious **tone**.

"Well yeah, why would I make something like that up?" Dale replied.

"Do you remember what day that happened, Dale?"

"Wow, let me think...it had to be on a Thursday because I only have time to go home for lunch on Mondays and Thursdays, and I remember it being closer to the end of the week."

"Was my grandfather here?" Debra asked urgently.

Dale scratched his head, trying to remember any other details. "Like I said, Debra, I was driving back to school after my lunch, and

I was surprised to see a Salvation Army truck in his driveway moving his **piano**. I didn't see anyone else, and I thought I should check in with Mr. Herman to see what gives. Debra, I hope I haven't done anything wrong, and I'm not trying to be nosy."

"Dale, you are wonderful! We thought someone stole his **player piano**, and until now, we haven't had any information to go on! You are a lifesaver! You've given us a **lead** to follow up on! Thanks so much!"

"Does that mean you'll go out with me now, Debra?" Dale asked with a slight grin on his face.

"Don't push your luck, Dale!" she replied with a giggle.

"I figured you'd say that, but you can't blame a guy for trying!"

When Dale had gone, Debra ran back downstairs to the **music** room and summoned **Middle C**.

"This is a surprise, Debra. Did you forget something?" **Middle C** asked.

"Oh my goodness, Mr. **Middle C**, I just found out something extremely important about my grandfather's missing **player piano**!"

"What, dear girl? Do tell me at once."

Debra hurried to relay the information she had received from Dale.

"Very interesting indeed. It's too bad that he didn't see anyone else but the Salvation Army personnel. Be that as it may, we still have a valuable clue to go off of."

"I can't wait until my grandfather gets home so I can give him the good news!" Debra informed **Middle C** excitedly.

"Debra, I must ask you not to say a word to him at this time."

"But why, Mr. **Middle C**? He's been so depressed."

"For the very fact that Dale didn't see the real culprit who's behind all this. We can do our own investigation first and find out who initiated this whole process. If we let the cat out of the bag too early, and Mildred or Rita get wind of it, they could contact the Salvation Army first, causing a cover up of their involvement."

"Oh, wow…I didn't even stop to think about that. I'm so grateful that I was the only one home when Dale came to the door, so we can get a head start on this whole situation. Thank you, Mr. **Middle C**, I don't know what I would do without you!"

For the next few minutes, **Middle C** outlined a plan for Debra to follow on what she needed to do, with a promise that she would only communicate the results to Ted or himself. Waving goodbye, she went back upstairs to make sure the house was in order before preparing to leave. Finding everything as it should be, she picked up the money from the kitchen table, locked the front door, and hurried down the stairs to her car.

It was difficult not to say anything to her mother about the new developments on the missing **player piano** when she got home; however, she did promise **Middle C**, and she was a girl of her word. After picking up the Martins' ironing, she went downstairs and tried to call Ted. She was frustrated to hear that she had just barely missed him, having left for work a few minutes earlier, and he wouldn't be home until late. She might as well just settle into her ironing because she couldn't talk to anyone in her family about the situation and Ted would be working all night. She hoped there was a good movie on TV so it would take her mind off all the things that were going through her head!

Mildred had spent a pleasant day with Paul and she was relieved to see that he had settled down from the loss of his **player piano**. They went on their morning walk together, and Paul had offered to take her out to a weekend brunch, which was a real treat. When she had seen Debra's car parked at Paul's house, she thought for sure she would be in for an interrogation on the missing **player piano**. Fortunately for both of them, Debra had been downstairs doing the wash, and she and Paul were able to slip out the front door before having to come face-to-face with her. If Mildred had her way, things would continue on the way they had today, and soon the **player piano** would be just a distant memory!

Rita was having a temper tantrum, throwing anything she could get her hands on in her bedroom. Her mother had sent a maid to her room to try to settle her down; however, the maid was successful at only becoming a target for Rita to take her rage out on. Rita still couldn't accept the fact that Ted had feelings for such a plain and nothing country bumpkin. Was he crazy, when he could have someone of her caliber? Then there was the fact that neither Angie nor Mildred would pick up the telephone when she called. Things better start changing, and they needed to change *now*!

Chapter 15

Monday afternoon found Debra busy doing homework, which was a huge challenge for her, especially after the information she had just received from the Salvation Army. She wished Ted would give her a call because she was going out of her mind needing to talk to someone! Her thoughts were interrupted by the ringing of the telephone, and she raced to answer it.

"Hello."

"Debra, is that you?" Ted asked.

"Yes, it is, Ted, and am I glad to hear your **voice**. You may want to sit down while I tell you the latest." She quickly brought him up to date and then told him about her latest conversation with the Salvation Army. "I just got off the phone with a Mr. Beckon, and he pulled all the paperwork from the day they picked up the **player piano** from my grandfather's house. He advised me that the request was placed by a woman, and they just assumed it was 'Mrs. Herman' placing the request. Nothing was signed by anyone the day they picked it up, but as soon as the trucks come in for the night, they are going to meet with the guys that picked up the **player piano** to see if they can get a description of the woman. What do you want to bet it will be Mildred or Rita?"

"Wow…good work, Debra! This is amazing how it's all coming together. If I had to guess, I would guess it's Rita that did it. Wasn't Mildred on vacation with your grandfather then?"

"You're right, Ted, I had forgotten about that, which reminds me, I better have them verify the day and time it was picked up so we accuse the right person."

"Well, I do have some good news for you too! I was able to get the Saturday before Halloween off!"

"Oh, Ted, that is good news! I can't wait to spend the whole day with you! Wow, everything good is coming together for us, isn't it?"

"Yes, and it's about time, don't you think?"

"Definitely. Once we find out who did this, then you and I and **Middle C** need to meet to figure out what our next step will be. I hope to hear back from Mr. Beckon in a day or so. If not, I will give him a call."

"I'll look forward to your next call. I still want you to be careful, Debra. I would have never guessed that someone would steal your grandfather's **player piano**, so whoever it is will get desperate if they suspect we're on to them. Promise me you'll keep **Middle C** and I informed of your whereabouts so we can help you if trouble comes your way."

"I promise I will, Ted, and thanks for caring."

Debra felt a little nervous about everything after considering Ted's words. She would have never gone to the lengths that someone had gone to to steal a **piano**, so she could only imagine what that same person would do if they had any idea of how close they were getting to identifying them.

Debra spent time after dinner **practicing** her **recital piece**; however, her mind was so preoccupied with who stole her grandfather's **player piano** that it was next to impossible to memorize a single section of her **piece**. Finally surrendering to her thoughts, she just focused on **practicing** the **song** and adding the **dynamics** where indicated.

The week was dragging by as she waited anxiously to hear back from the Salvation Army. By Thursday afternoon, she decided she had waited long enough for an answer and placed a call to Mr. Beckon.

"Mr. Beckon, this is Debra Wilkin. I called a few days ago and spoke to you about the Salvation Army picking up an old **player piano** from my grandfather's home. You were going to check with your personnel to see if you could get a description of the woman that placed the request. I really need this information, and I'm following up to see what you've found out."

"Oh yes, Miss Wilkin. I did have a chance to speak to the men who picked up the **piano**. They mentioned that she was an older woman, very agitated and in a great hurry to get them in and out."

"Can you give me any more details on what she looked like—color of her hair, whether she was heavy set, etc.?" Debra asked.

"Well, they said she had gray hair, small-to-average build, and kept complaining that they needed to hurry because she had other things she needed to do that day."

"That description definitely gives me a little more to go on. Lastly, Mr. Beckon, could you please tell me the day and time the **piano** was picked up by the Salvation Army?"

"Yes, it was Thursday, September 12, and the appointment time was 12:00 p.m."

"Thank you, Mr. Beckon. My last question is, where is the **piano** now, and can we **arrange** to get it back? You see, Mr. Beckon, that woman did not have my grandfather's permission to take the **player piano**, and he is very anxious to get it back."

"I was afraid you were going to say that, and that's part of the reason I was slow in returning your phone call. We have put out several tracers on the **piano** and are still in the process of trying to locate its whereabouts. We will continue our pursuit to try to retrieve it, and as soon as I have an update for you, I will call back immediately."

Debra hung up the phone and felt positive that the woman Mr. Beckon described was Mildred, but how was that possible when she was on vacation with her grandfather? Something wasn't adding up! She called Ted; however, he wasn't home and his mother wasn't sure what time he would be back. Somehow she needed to question her grandfather about Mildred's possible involvement without him becoming suspicious. That wasn't going to be easy, but she had to get to the bottom of this!

Debra didn't sleep very well Friday night and woke up early Saturday morning. She tried putting herself into a detective role to see if she could come up with some clues about Mildred. The only details she could come up with about Mildred were the following: she is very self-centered, she couldn't care less about her grandfather's interest in **music**, and she always has a migraine headache whenever she needs an excuse to get out of something. "Well, I guess I wouldn't be a very good detective because none of these three things add up to much."

She hurried to get dressed and kept trying to come up with more ideas that would make sense about Mildred's possible involvement. When she arrived at her grandfather's house, she realized she had never talked to him about his vacation with Mildred; instead, they had mainly talked about his missing **player piano**. It might be a good idea to take some time before she started cleaning to **learn** more about his vacation.

"Good morning, Grandpa! How are you doing?"

"I'm doing great! Come in, Debra! How about a glass of orange juice. Do you have time this morning?"

"I certainly do, Grandpa. I was thinking on my drive over that I never got to hear about your vacation last week. We mainly just talked about your missing **piano**. Would you like to talk about it?"

"Yes…that would be nice. I'm not in a hurry this morning either. Mildred called earlier and said she has one of her migraines and won't be able to walk today."

Debra perked up when he mentioned Mildred having a migraine and thought this was a perfect time to question her grandfather about them. "Oh, that's too bad. She sure has a lot of migraines, doesn't she?"

"Yes, she does. As a matter of fact, she had one on the Thursday we were supposed to leave on our vacation. She called me early that morning and told me she would have to make **arrangements** to fly out to West Virginia Friday night. I told her I would wait and fly with her, but she insisted I go ahead, not wanting to ruin my vacation. She sure is thoughtful, isn't she?"

"Ohhh, very thoughtful!" Debra couldn't believe she had just hit the jackpot and could now nail Mildred! She might make a good detective after all. After **listening** to her grandfather's monologue of vacation events, the pieces of the puzzle were finally coming together, and Mildred was definitely in the center of all the trouble. It took every ounce of control she had not to blurt out the truth, but she had promised Ted and **Middle C** she wouldn't, so she sat still while biting her tongue.

"Well, my dear, as you can see, I could talk your **ear** off all day. I better let you get some work done."

"You know I love hearing about all of your adventures, Grandpa! But you're right, I better get your wash started, and then I'm going to summon **Middle C**. Leave me a list of what you need done today and I will do it." She stood up and gave him a hug, happy to know it wouldn't be long before she could tell him the truth about Mildred.

Debra was so anxious to summon **Middle C** that she practically flew down the stairs. Her grandfather had placed some dirty clothes in the washroom, so she quickly sorted through them and started the first load. It didn't take long after that to summon **Middle C**.

"Mr. **Middle C**, I thought you'd never get here. I've solved the mystery of the stolen **player piano** and can't wait to tell you and Ted all about it!"

"Well, in that case, let's be off." And he hurried to dial his **metronome** to the proper settings.

Ted was a little confused about why **Middle C** had landed the **music** mobile in the parking lot across the street from his **rest** stop and walked over to see what the problem was. "Hey, **Middle C**, is everything okay? How come you didn't pick me up where you normally do?"

"Come in, Ted, Debra has some news and I thought we should all discuss it before arriving at the **conservatory**."

Debra brought them quickly up to date on her phone call with Mr. Beckon from the Salvation Army and her latest conversation with her grandfather where he unknowingly explained how and when Mildred was able to **orchestrate** the disposal of the **player piano**.

"Wow, and all this time I thought for sure it was Rita that had stolen the **player piano**," Ted replied, still puzzled.

"Didn't I tell you not to underestimate Mildred?" Debra said with a knowing expression. "I'm telling you, that woman is deadly!"

"And don't you forget that, Debra!" **Middle C** stated. "We now know what she is capable of doing, so you must be doubly careful and alert for whatever her next move will be."

They spent the next few minutes reviewing several strategies on how to expose Mildred, trying to choose the safest plan for everyone involved. Checking his watch, **Middle C** announced it was time that they leave for the **conservatory**.

Debra's mind was so preoccupied with Mildred's involvement in stealing her grandfather's **player piano** that it was difficult for her to pay attention to Brenda's **instructions**. She could tell that she had disappointed her instructor after she finished **playing** her **recital piece**, especially without any of the passages being committed to memory. "I promise I will find more time this week to **practice**, Brenda, and I will come back next week better prepared, with several sections memorized."

"I just don't want you to miss out on any of the upcoming opportunities, Debra, and I know you will if you're not more prepared," Brenda stated.

When she and Ted were flying back on the **music** mobile, Ted could see that Debra was unhappy about something. "I wish you would tell me what you're so down about, Debra."

"I'm embarrassed to say I let Brenda down by not having part of my **recital piece** memorized. I've been so preoccupied with the situation with my grandfather's **player piano** and Mildred, I couldn't focus on my **music**."

"Hey, sweetie, that's only temporary. We now know who did it, and soon she'll be put away and things will return to normal. You'll have your **recital piece memorized** in no time."

"You're right, Ted. It just felt awful to disappoint her."

After landing at Ted's **rest** stop, he kissed Debra goodbye and said, "We have a lot of fun things to look forward to. I get to come to your fall carnival and dance, your grandfather's going to get his

player piano back, and things are looking up for us. I need to see that beautiful smile of yours, Debra."

She rewarded him with a brilliant smile and said, "You're right, Ted. Thanks for your patience, and I promise to be more cheerful the next time we're together."

"Well, it won't be long. Next weekend is the carnival, and we'll be closing the case of the missing **player piano**, starring Mildred, this week."

Debra was in deep thought the **rest** of the flight back to her grandfather's home, worried about how he would react when he heard about Mildred's involvement with his **player piano**.

When they landed, **Middle C** turned to her and said, "I'm sorry things turned out this way, Debra, but your grandfather has to know the truth, and I'll be here to support you while you tell him."

"I know. I just don't want to hurt him."

"Think about the pain we're saving him from now and in his future by telling him the truth today."

"Okay, I'll go and get him." Debra took a deep breath and slowly went upstairs to get her grandfather.

"Hello, Debra, how was your day at the **conservatory**?" he asked after she had opened the door to the kitchen.

"It went pretty good. Grandpa, **Middle C** and I would like to talk to you for a few minutes."

"Okay, from the look on your face, it **sounds** pretty serious."

She didn't dare open her mouth; instead, she turned and began walking down the stairs. She couldn't believe how hard her heart was pounding and how shaky her legs were as she took each step back down to the **music** room.

"Hello, Paul," **Middle C** greeted as they walked into the room.

"It's good to see you, **Middle C**. I can't thank you enough for giving Debra another way to summon you after my **player piano** got stolen."

"I was upset, too, when I heard about your **player piano**. That's one of the things Debra and I wanted to talk to you about today. She was able to do a little investigating and has come up with some answers I think you need to hear."

Paul quickly turned to her and said, "Is that true, Debra? You know who stole my **player piano**?"

Debra nodded her head and quietly brought her grandfather up to date on the visit from Dale to the phone conversations with the Salvation Army, all pointing the finger at Mildred's involvement.

"I think I better sit down before I fall down," Paul replied in shock. "This is all so unbelievable! I don't even know what to think or say. I trusted her, and she betrayed me in the worst possible way!"

"We're sorry we had to be the bearer of such bad news, Paul. We need your cooperation this week in implementing her involvement in all of this. It's going to take a lot of patience and restraining of your temper in order to trap her into confessing her part in the stealing of your **player piano**. Are you willing to help us?"

"**Middle C**, I will do whatever's necessary. I can't believe I've been so blind, and I wish I would have **listened** to Debra's warnings. I'm sorry, Debra, will you ever forgive me?"

With tears streaming down her face, Debra ran to her grandfather and said, "Grandpa, there's nothing to forgive. I'm just so sorry you had to get hurt by all of this. I'm worried that you're going to be mad at me once all of this has been settled."

"No, my dear, I could never be mad at you for the choices I've made." Looking at **Middle C**, he said, "Let me know what you want me to do, **Middle C**, and I'll give you my full cooperation."

The next few days for Debra were difficult, especially not being able to say anything to her mother about Mildred's involvement in the disappearance of the **player piano**. Just when she thought things couldn't get any worse, she was on her way to a meeting after school about the fall carnival when Matt tapped her on the shoulder.

"Hey, slow down, perty girl, where's the fire?"

"Oh hello, Matt."

"Are you on your way to the meeting?" Matt asked.

"Yes."

"Good, so am I. I was hoping to catch you alone so I could ask you if you would spend the day with me at the carnival and dance the night away with me that night. I can't think of anyone else I would want to spend holding in my arms all day. What do you say, Strawberry?"

Debra's heart sank to her feet, and she felt miserable, not wanting to hurt his feelings. "Matt, I'm so sorry. I've already said I would spend the day with someone else."

"Who?" Matt asked, shocked.

"His name is Ted Nobson, a good friend I met over the summer."

"Oh. Well then…I hope y'all have fun, and I guess I better be quicker next time."

"Thanks for thinking of me, Matt."

"That's what I get for not thinking I have any competition. I should have known that a perty girl like you has a lot of beaus that are just waiting in line to take her out. It's okay, Miss Strawberry. I've certainly learned my lesson, and you can believe that I will start stepping up my game."

She watched him saunter away and didn't think she could feel any worse than she did now. This dating stuff was not easy and certainly not cracked up to what she thought it would be. She had always daydreamed of guys lining up vying for her attention; however, in her daydreams, she had never hurt anyone's feelings. "I never meant to hurt anyone's feelings," she mumbled.

"Whose feelings did you hurt?" Patty asked as she joined Debra.

"Matt's. He just asked me to spend the day with him at the carnival and dance, but I had to say no because I'm going with Ted."

"I thought you didn't know if Ted could go or not."

"I talked to him over the weekend, and he told me he had **arranged** to get the time off and will be flying up for the weekend."

"Wow, Debra, who would have thought you would have boy problems! Well, congratulations, girl! How do you like the world of popularity?"

"Right now it feels pretty awful. I hate hurting anyone's feelings."

"That's nonsense, girl! You should be enjoying the realization that guys are lining up for your attention. It could be worse, you know!"

Once again Debra was missing out on sleep thinking about hurting Matt's feelings and worrying about what was going to happen with Mildred when she had to face the **music** tomorrow about her part in the missing **player piano**. Before going to bed, she had called her grandfather to see if everything was ready for their confrontation. He had assured her it was; however, she could hear the misery in his **voice**. She couldn't help thinking about all the times she looked forward to Mildred getting what she deserved; however, now it wasn't nearly as rewarding as she thought it would be. Closing her eyes, she focused on shutting out all the troublesome thoughts of the world and concentrated all her energy into **resting**. Tomorrow was going to be a challenging day, and she needed to be at her best.

Chapter 16

Debra parked a block away from her grandfather's house and walked there in order not to alert Mildred of what was about to happen shortly. When she rounded the corner, she saw Dale going up the stairs to her grandfather's home.

"Thank you both for coming," her grandfather greeted after opening the front door. "Let's sit down and talk before Mildred arrives, and I will review with you what's going to happen." He explained that Mildred was coming over for lunch and had no idea that during their meal, the Salvation Army and the men who picked up the **player piano** would be paying them a visit. He would also invite Dale to join them so he could verify that he was the one who saw the Salvation Army picking up his **piano**. For now, he and Debra would wait in his bedroom until they were summoned.

Dale and Debra took their positions in her grandfather's bedroom while he checked on the chicken baking in the oven. After closing the oven door, the doorbell rang, and he said to no one in particular, "Show time."

"Well, hello, Paul. I can't tell you how nice it is to be invited to lunch," Mildred gushed. "It smells wonderful. Can I give you a hand with anything?"

"I think everything is ready. Follow me into the kitchen and let's sit down."

"The table looks beautiful, Paul. What a wonderful host you are."

"Have a seat, Mildred, while I pull the chicken out of the oven, and then we can get started." With the chicken **resting** on a hot plate on the table, Paul opened the refrigerator and reached for a fruit salad and some chilled glasses of water and lemon. After saying a blessing on the food, Paul told her to dig in. They had barely had a bite or two when the doorbell rang again. "Excuse me, Mildred, let me see who's at the door."

Mildred could hear Paul talking to some men but didn't think anything about it until she heard them mention something about a **player piano**. The hairs on the back of her neck began to stand up when Paul told them that she was in the kitchen and invited them to come and talk to her. When she saw them walk into the kitchen and recognized them as the men from the Salvation Army, she thought for sure her heart was going to give out right then and there!

"Mildred, these men are from the Salvation Army, and they said a woman called and requested that they come and dispose of my old **player piano**. I told them that I wasn't married and couldn't imagine who would do such a thing. They said they would remember the woman if they saw her and asked if they could come and see you." Turning to the men from the Salvation Army, Paul asked, "Gentlemen, is this the woman who made the request?"

The two men took a long look at Mildred and replied, "Yes, sir, she's the one that let us in."

"You two are lying," Mildred gasped in denial. "I've never seen you two in my life!"

"Excuse me, Mr. Herman, but I recognize her nasty **voice** too. The whole time we were trying to get your **piano** out of the basement, she kept complaining and squawking that we weren't working fast enough and she had other things she needed to do."

"And just when did I supposedly request you to come and pick up a **piano**? You two are crazy. I was out of town on vacation with you, Paul. I can't believe you're **listening** to these two liars."

"Wait right here, gentlemen." Paul stepped out of the kitchen and into the living room area and called for Dale.

"Yes, Mr. Herman," Dale said as he walked around the corner.

"Could you verify for me that these two men are the ones you saw that day from the Salvation Army?"

Dale took a good look at them and also went to the front window to look at their truck. Turning back, he said, "Yes Mr. Herman, these are the men, and they were driving a truck that looked exactly like the one parked out front the day I saw them loading your **piano** into it."

"Paul, when did all of this happen? Aren't you forgetting we were in West Virginia?"

"Gentlemen, please give me the day of the week and the time you came to pick up the **piano**."

"We had an appointment on Thursday, September 12, at 12:00 p.m. **sharp**."

Paul turned to Mildred and said, "Mildred, if you'll remember, you called me early that Thursday morning and advised me that you had a migraine and wouldn't be able to go with me but would meet me in West Virginia on Friday night. I went ahead and left, and while I was gone, apparently you **arranged** to have my **player piano** picked up. Why would you do that?"

"Because I hate your granddaughter Debra and that horrible girl, Rita, who kept threatening me if I didn't do it. It's all their fault, Paul, can't you see that?"

"Mildred, I think it's time you left, and I don't want to see you or have anything to do with you ever again."

"Mr. Herman, do you want us to press charges or call the police on her?" the men from the Salvation Army asked.

"Well, I never," Mildred said, hurrying to get to the front door before anyone was the wiser.

"Mr. Herman, Mildred is getting away. Do you want me to grab her?" Dale asked.

"No, just let her go. I don't really want to press charges either. If I get my **player piano** back, I'll be happy. I'd prefer not to have to talk or deal with her anymore."

"Mr. Beckon told us to tell you he's still working on getting the location of where your **piano** was taken. I'm sure he'll call you as soon as he has all the details. Do you need anything else from us?"

"No, you two can go. I do appreciate your stopping by so you could positively identify her as the woman who let you in. By the way, was she in my house when you came to pick up the **piano**?"

"Yes, she answered the front door when we rang the doorbell."

"Wow…now I'm curious as to how she got a **key** to my house. I better have the locks on my house changed. I don't want to worry about her getting back in again."

Debra and Dale watched the men from the Salvation Army leave. "Dale, I appreciate you spending your lunch hour here so you could positively identify everyone you saw a few weeks ago."

"I was happy to do it, Mr. Herman. I'm sorry it ended the way it did for you."

"It could have been a lot worse, Dale. I'm just grateful no one was hurt."

"I probably ought to be going now," Dale said. "If you need anything else, just let me know."

After Dale left, Debra asked, "Are you going to be okay, Grandpa?"

"Yes, it'll just take some time. I'm still in a little bit of shock that Mildred would do something like that. I really thought she was someone special. Love can be very blind at times."

"Don't be so hard on yourself, Grandpa. Are you going to change the locks on your house today?"

"I think I better, don't you? I'm still curious about how she got a **key** to my house, but not curious enough to ask her. Now you, dear girl, better get to school before I get in trouble with them and your mother. I'll call your mother today and explain everything so she'll know why you had to keep it from her."

Debra walked over to her grandfather and gave him a big hug and then picked up her purse to leave. "I'll see you Saturday morning, Grandpa. I love you."

"I love you too, Debra."

Mildred was in a panic and on the phone, trying to explain to Rita what had just happened at Paul's house.

"I should have known better than to trust a bumbling idiot like you to do the job right! Honestly, Mildred, why did you all but confess your involvement?"

"You weren't there, Rita, they cornered me by bringing those two men from the Salvation Army over to positively identify me. What else was I supposed to do? They even verified the date and time, which jogged Paul's memory into reminding him that I didn't leave on vacation with him, but flew to where he was the next evening. I'm so scared they're going to throw me in jail. Oh, what's to become of me?" Mildred moaned pitifully.

"Oh, for goodness' sake, Mildred, get a hold of yourself! You're too old and crotchety to go to jail! You may have to do some community service but nothing too drastic. You should be concerned about how all of this is going to affect me! You didn't mention my name, did you?"

There was a long **pause** of **silence**, followed by Rita yelling into the phone, "You did mention my name, didn't you? I should have known I could never trust an old bat like you. Well just get this through that thick skull of yours—if I go down, you'll go down! You got that?" More **silence** followed, and Rita, losing her temper, slammed the phone back into its receiver.

When Debra got home from school, her mother called to her, letting her know she was in the kitchen. Something smelled heavenly; sitting on the table were freshly baked chocolate chip cookies. "I figured you needed a treat today, and, I made your favorite. Why don't you pull up a chair, grab a cookie and some milk, and let's have a nice long chat."

It felt good to be able to talk to her mother and share her innermost feelings about all she had been going through the past few days, excluding of course, anything to do with **Middle C** and the **conservatory**.

"Grandpa told me all about how you put the pieces together and solved the case of his missing **player piano**. I'm so proud of you, Debra! I'm sorry you had to keep it all to yourself for a few days, but now that everything's out in the open, I understand. I am worried about you, dear. Are you going to be okay?"

"I think so. I thought I would be so happy to see Mildred get what she deserved, but I saw how much it hurt Grandpa, and it didn't make me very happy after all. Pretty confusing, huh?"

"Justice and vengeance aren't always what they're cracked up to be, are they? It's not easy to see someone pay for their consequences, even when they deserve it.

Rita summoned her **mediator**, **Largo**, to pick her up to go to the **conservatory** earlier than usual on Saturday morning. "You're probably wondering, **Largo**, why I summoned you here so early. I've been thinking about you a lot lately and wanted to thank you for all the kind things you've done for me over the past months since we've become acquainted. I hope you won't think I'm being forward when I ask you this question. Do you have a girlfriend?"

Largo blushed with embarrassment and then cleared his throat and replied, "Yes, her name is **Melody**."

"**Melody**, what a beautiful name and so appropriate for you," Rita cooed with excitement. "Well, I would like to reward you with an all-expense-paid night out on the town for one teeny tiny favor."

"I don't know about that, Rita. I'm not supposed to do anything other than my job description."

"Oh, **Largo**, you're always worrying and thinking the worst about me. You know I would never ask you to do anything to jeopardize your position here. When are you going to start trusting me?"

"Well, just what did you have in mind?"

"You know my good friend Debra at the **conservatory**? Her birthday is coming up soon, and I am planning a wonderful surprise birthday party for her! I need your help in kidnapping her and then bringing her to me so I can take her to a restaurant I have reserved where a group of her closest friends will be waiting to surprise her. Doesn't that **sound** like fun, **Largo**?"

"Yeah, I guess so."

"After you bring her to me, I will hand you prepaid tickets and reservations for a night out on the town, and then you and **Melody** can enjoy an unforgettable evening together! Here's what I have in mind, and this is what I need you to do."

The crisp fall air felt good on Debra's drive over to her grandfather's house. She was excited about the day ahead and couldn't wait to enjoy all the fun activities the day had in store. Her grandfather had even called the night before to tell her tomorrow was officially a holiday for her after all she had been through. She had tried to object; however, he reminded her in no uncertain terms that he was the boss. She couldn't help laughing, and ended their call by reminding him how much she loved him.

"Good morning Debra! Come in, my dear girl!"

"You are in a lot better mood than I thought you'd be in after all you've gone through, Grandpa!"

"Well, it doesn't do a lot of good to sit around feeling sorry for myself. The busier I am, the happier I am."

"Did you change your locks?"

"Yes, I took care of that on Thursday shortly after you left. I'm also keeping busy by crafting a new **violin**, and when I get tired of doing that, I **practice** the **organ** or my **harmonica**."

"I'm happy to see that you are staying busy and not moping. When I get back from the **conservatory** today, I will have Ted with me, and you can finally meet him, Grandpa. He's going to the fall carnival with me this afternoon and the dance tonight."

"Well, I can see that you have an exciting day to look forward to. I will enjoy meeting your young man and will be here working on something when you return."

Waving goodbye, she hurried downstairs and quickly summoned **Middle C**, eager to get her day started. When they arrived at Ted's **rest** stop, it seemed like Ted looked more handsome than usual, if that were possible, and she noticed that he carried a suit and an extra change of clothes. "Good morning, Debra," he said and leaned over to give her a kiss.

"Hello to you, handsome! I can't wait to spend the day with you!"

"That makes two of us! I still can't believe my manager gave me the day off, but I'm not going to complain or he may change his mind! Before we get to the **conservatory**, I want to know if you're doing okay after your ordeal on Thursday with Mildred."

"I have to admit I've been surprised at the emotions I've gone through, Ted. I thought I would really be happy to see Mildred fall off her high and mighty pedestal, but to tell you the truth, I've been sad and a little depressed over the whole situation. I saw how much this whole thing hurt my grandfather, and it's made me sad and kind of depressed. I wish Mildred could have been the special lady he hoped she was instead of the jealous monster she is. He's putting on a good front and trying his best to move forward, but I'm still worried about him."

"That's understandable. I'm looking forward to meeting your grandfather today."

"He's anxious to meet you too, Ted. I hope you'll take the time to **sing** something for him. He loves **music**, and it'll make a great impression on him! I've told him all about your incredible **voice**!"

"Well, in that case, consider it a done deal."

They landed at the **conservatory**, and both hurried to class knowing when they were finished they could begin their fun afternoon and evening. With everything that had gone down lately, they didn't pay much attention to Rita; however, she watched their every move, smiling inwardly at her plans for the unsuspecting couple!

"I'm so anxious to get back to my grandfather's house so you two can meet!" Debra said happily on their way back from the **conservatory**.

"It feels a little strange not being dropped off at my **rest** stop."

Soon they felt the slight jolt of their landing, and they knew they had arrived at their destination. "Well, my two **students**, you have a wonderful day together, and I'll pick you up later, Ted, when you summon me. Don't forget to squeeze some time in this week for your **music**. I'll see you next Saturday, Debra," **Middle C** said while waving goodbye.

"I still can't get over your grandfather's collection of hats. I wish we had more time so I could get a little history on each one."

"Whatever you do, don't mention them, or we'll never get out of this house to go to the carnival or dance!" Debra led the way upstairs, and the closer they got to the kitchen, the more they could smell the delicious aroma of homemade chili. Opening the door, they found Debra's grandfather standing by the stove stirring his appetizing chili.

"We're back, Grandpa!"

"So I see, and I hope you're hungry."

"I don't know of anyone that can resist the delicious aroma of your homemade chili, Grandpa. Before I forget, I want to introduce you to Ted."

"I am certainly pleased to meet you, Ted. Debra has told me about your amazing **talent**, and I'm hoping you will favor me with a **song** or two."

"I would love to, but only if you will **play** a **song** for me on your **harmonica** and **organ**."

"You strike a hard bargain, Ted, but one that I think we can come to terms with," Paul replied with a chuckle.

After lunch, Paul got out his **harmonica** and began to **play** several familiar **tunes**, and before long Ted joined in **singing** while Paul **played**. Debra wished she had a tape recorder and had to wipe away a few tears as she watched and **listened** to two very important men in her life. When the **song** ended, Paul said, "Debra certainly didn't exaggerate when she told me you have an amazing **voice**. I could **listen** to you all day and then some," Paul complimented Ted.

"Well, thank you! You have quite the **talent** for the **harmonica** as well!"

The next hour and a half was spent cleaning the kitchen and sharing their **musical talents** with each other, along with Debra's **performance** of the passages of her **recital piece** that she had **memorized**. Checking the time, Debra announced that they better change their clothes and be on their way.

It didn't take long to arrive at the carnival, and it was bustling with activity. "I'm so glad you'll get to meet a lot of my friends," Debra said happily. She reached into her back seat and pulled out the poster she had made for the bobbing for apples booth. "Our first stop will be at the booth I've been helping with."

Patty and Mike were working at the booth when Debra and Ted arrived. After introductions were made, Patty invited Ted to bob for an apple. While Ted was bobbing, Patty whispered to Debra, "You didn't tell me he was so good looking. No wonder you're crazy about him!"

"Yes, he is good looking, but he's also not stuck up about it, and he's a great guy to be around."

"I have to admit if I wasn't going with Mike, I might chase after him myself," Patty said with a longing look.

"All I have to say to that is thank heavens you're going with Mike!"

Their conversation was interrupted when Mike announced, "We have a winner! Let's give a round of **applause** to Ted, who caught an apple with his bare teeth!"

Debra couldn't help chuckling when she saw how drenched his face and shirt were from trying to nab an apple with his teeth, but nonetheless, he still looked charming! His win earned them a treat to some cotton candy, so they wandered off in that direction to collect on it!

Rita was tapping her foot while she waited impatiently for **Largo** to meet her at their prearranged rendezvous. It seemed like her whole future was riding on his arrival, and she was about to go crazy waiting for him. When she thought she couldn't wait a second longer, she was rewarded with the familiar **sound** of his arrival. Putting aside her temper, she said, "It's good to see you, **Largo**! You can't imagine how excited I am to surprise Debra for her birthday. Let's review our plan one more time just to make sure we're both on the same page."

After several minutes of going over every detail, **Largo** replied, "Okay, Rita, now you show me the tickets you purchased for **Melody** and I, and then I'll be on my way to pick up Debra."

"What...you don't trust me, **Largo**?" Rita asked in shock, which quickly turned to anger. No one had ever questioned her integrity before. Reaching into her bag, she pulled out the envelope that contained the tickets and showed them to **Largo**. "Now what do you have to say?"

"It's time for me to go and pick up Debra." With a quick snap of his fingers, **musical notes** began appearing, and within seconds **Largo** had vanished.

"**Largo** doesn't know how lucky he is that I need him to bring me the country bumpkin or he might have been **singing** a new **tune** about now. How dare he question my integrity! I have half a mind to teach him and his little **Melody** a valuable **lesson** when they get back!"

Debra couldn't remember the last time she had had such an enjoyable day. Her arms were now full of stuffed animals Ted had won for her at the various carnival booths. Not only could he **sing** amazingly, he was also very adept and skilled when it came to competing in all the games being offered. "I am the luckiest girl on earth to be with you, Ted. I've always had a secret desire to go to a carnival with a guy who could win all of these fantastic stuffed animals for me! You're the best, Ted. You've made my dream come true! Thank you so much for being here and making it all so fun!"

"It's my pleasure, Debra. I love seeing you so happy. It's a nice change from all the headaches you've had to endure lately," he said, giving her a hug and a kiss.

"Oh, you mean those 'migraines,' as in Mildred?"

"All right, smarty-pants, you got me on that one," he said, laughing. "I think we need to go back to your car and put some of these animals away. If I keep winning, pretty soon you'll be covered up, and I'll have to dig through stuffed animals to find you!"

After depositing her precious cargo into the backseat of her car, they decided to grab a snack. Ted went and got in line, and Debra grabbed a seat at a table, reserving a spot for them to sit. While she was waiting for Ted, she thought she heard someone call her name and turned around to see **Largo** walking toward her. "Hello, **Largo**, what on earth are you doing here?" she asked curiously.

"You're never going to believe this. My girlfriend, **Melody**, and I have tickets to see a **play** today, and we plan to go to dinner after the **play**. I was on my way to pick up **Melody** and I started having trouble with my **music** mobile and decided to land in the grassy area where I wouldn't be noticed. After landing, I happened to see you and thought I would check to see if you have a flashlight I could borrow."

"Yes, I do have a flashlight in my car. I'm here with Ted, and he's in line getting us some food. Let me walk over and tell him what's going on, and then we can go and get the flashlight. It didn't take long to inform Ted of what was happening, and he turned briefly to wave at **Largo**.

As Debra leaned into her car to pull the flashlight from her glovebox, she suddenly smelled something sweet, and the last thing she remembered was a cloth being pressed against her nose and the sensation of being dizzy.

"That's a girl. Just relax and let **Largo** carry you back to the **music** mobile, where you can have a nice little nap while I fly you to your surprise birthday party."

Rita was still miffed from her earlier conversation with **Largo**; however, if he delivered Debra to her, she could possibly get over her irritated feelings toward him. Her thoughts were unexpectedly interrupted when she heard the **sound** of his **music** mobile landing. Walking to meet it and seeing Debra lying unconscious, she said, "Nicely done, **Largo**. Now, if you'll carry her to my car, I'll give you your tickets, and you and **Melody** can enjoy the **rest** of your day."

Once Rita was settled into her car, she couldn't help smiling at her superiority, congratulating herself on a well thought out plan that was executed perfectly. She was finally in charge of the bothersome country bumpkin, and now she would have to answer to her authority! It felt incredible to be in this **arrangement**, and it even overwhelmed her and without realizing it, her wicked laugh escaped her lips, sending the alarming **sound** into the subconscious mind of Debra causing her to shudder.

Where am I? Debra wondered. *What am I supposed to be doing?* Her mind was so foggy, with the last memory of being with Ted and holding tons of stuffed animals. Why was she holding so many stuffed animals? Things were getting a little clearer. She suddenly remembered being at the carnival. Her stomached growled, and she remembered being hungry and Ted was in line, buying them a snack. Why was it taking so long? Why couldn't she remember? She was at a table, and she heard her name. Who was calling her name? She remembered seeing **Largo**, and then there was that sweet smell…and everything got dizzy. Now she could hear a vicious and cruel laugh that **sounded** vaguely familiar. She had heard that laugh before, but where? She sensed she was moving, but she wasn't sure where she was going. There was that obnoxious laugh again, and now she remembered who it belonged to—Rita!

Oh no, this had to be a terrible nightmare. Please tell me this isn't happening. I need to wake up right now!

When she opened her eyes, everything seemed fuzzy, and she didn't recognize where she was or anything familiar about her surroundings. She could still feel the sensation of moving and decided she was in a car with **Largo** or Rita, or possibly both. She knew she had heard Rita's laugh, but she could only remember seeing **Largo**. Somehow, he was involved with Rita's plan. Oh, why did she have to trust him, especially when she was having such a perfect day with Ted? She felt the car slowing down and decided the best thing for her to do now would be to pretend she was still out of it until she could figure out what they had in store for her.

Rita put the car in park and turned around to look at Debra, saying, "I bet you wish you were Sleeping Beauty instead of the bothersome country bumpkin. Well, sleep on 'cause you're going to need all the beauty sleep you can get where you're going!"

Continued in book 3

CPSIA information can be obtained
at www.ICGtesting.com
Printed in the USA
BVHW070221101118
532734BV00001B/39/P

9 781643 451435